ON A SCALE FROM IDIOT TO COMPLETE JERK

⟶ A Highly Scientific Study
of Annoying Behavior

Science Project by J.J. Murphy*

*with
Alison Hughes

Library and Archives Canada Cataloguing in Publication

Hughes, Alison, 1966-, author
On a scale from idiot to complete jerk / Alison Hughes.

Issued in print and electronic formats.
ISBN 978-1-4598-0484-5 (pbk.).--ISBN 978-1-4598-0485-2 (pdf).--
ISBN 978-1-4598-0486-9 (epub)

I. Title.
PS8615.U316505 2014   jc813'.6   C2013-906648-9
C2013-906649-7

First published in the United States, 2014
Library of Congress Control Number: 2013954114

Summary: J.J.'s science report has everything: graphs, charts, case studies,
a quiz and the best subject matter of all time—jerks (and a few idiots).

*Orca Book Publishers is dedicated to preserving the environment and
has printed this book on Forest Stewardship Council® certified paper.*

Orca Book Publishers gratefully acknowledges the support for its publishing
programs provided by the following agencies: the Government of Canada through
the Canada Book Fund and the Canada Council for the Arts, and the Province of British
Columbia through the BC Arts Council and the Book Publishing Tax Credit.

Design and illustrations by Jenn Playford
Cover image by Dreamstime; Cover illustrations by Jenn Playford
Author photo by Barbara Heintzman

ORCA BOOK PUBLISHERS   ORCA BOOK PUBLISHERS
PO Box 5626, Stn. B   PO Box 468
Victoria, BC Canada   Custer, WA USA
V8R 6S4   98240-0468

www.orcabook.com
Printed and bound in Canada.

17 16 15 14 • 4 3 2 1

To M, for everything.
And to Gig, for somehow making us love him
despite being a bit of a jerk.

On a Scale from Idiot to Complete Jerk

A Highly Scientific Study of Annoying Behavior

Science Project by **J.J. Murphy**

CONTENTS

CHAPTER 1
The Dawn of the Jerk

Imagine a very different world, billions of years ago. Okay, probably more like millions. Millions of years ago, nothing was as we now know it. There were no buildings, cars, airplanes, roads or electric lights. There was no pizza, and even if there had been, there were no ovens to cook it in. There were no wheels, paper, clothes or shoes, let alone computers, TVs or cell phones. There were no science projects, because there was no science class (or schools or grades or paper).

Earth was a wild, creepy place. There were oceans practically everywhere, and only one big, really weird-looking piece of land. Roaring volcanoes spewed lava and fossilized all the things that died. Monster birdlike thingies screeched and soared over the vast ocean and the forests of enormous ferns. Strange animals scrabbled out a living on land. It was a tough life, one where a creature didn't know if it would be alive that night to sleep with one eye open for predators. The animals with flattish teeth grazed on plants. Those with pointy teeth ate the plant grazers. It was all pretty logical.

But all of a sudden one millennium, strange humanlike animals appeared, loping gorilla-style on all fours. These animals were pretty smart compared to the bacteria and algae that came before them. They started grunting at each other, using rocks for tools, and drawing on cave walls. And instead of all the humanlike things fending for themselves, they figured in their smallish, flat heads, *Hey, if we all stick together, we'll be harder to kill*. And they were.

Problem time. Even if you don't become some prehistoric monster's lunch, living together sometimes sucks. Because not all people, even those early, grunting, ape-walking humans, are nice. Newly discovered cave scratchings show us this. (They can't really be called drawings because they're pretty bad. Think of your two-year-old cousin holding up a paper and screaming, "IT'S A CAT!" which you would never have figured out *ever* without her telling you.)

These cave scratchings were found in a cave, obviously, in remote Bmugwanaland in June of this year. All the best cave-scratch experts say they tell an important story, rather than just being random doodles by a bored early human stuck in the cave on a long rainy day.

It's been in all the papers. Here's a bit from one of the articles:

The recent discovery in the Bmugwanaland caves of Central Africa continues to provoke discussion and debate among scientists.

"Yes, yes, they may look like the rudimentary scratchings of a demented two-year-old," said an irritated Professor Basil Worthington-Smythe, lead archaeologist of the scientific expedition.

"But," he added, "they very likely were scratched by an adolescent early human, possibly twelve to fourteen years old. And they clearly, unmistakably, paint a picture of a crucially important historical event."

Here's the story the cave scratchings tell. Once upon a time, a *very* long time ago, there was a small humanlike animal. He was all excited because he had found a really big, sturdy stick. You'd be pretty excited, too, if you'd seen the teeth on some of those monster predators. Anyway, so this little guy has a stick he's all proud of. He walks around with it. He props it against a rock. He shows off a bit with it. It's probably his only possession, other than possibly the rock.

But wait! A bigger humanlike animal struts over and swipes the little guy's stick! Just like that, he grabs it before the little guy even has a chance to crack him a good one with it. The bigger guy, with a weird, scratched "ha-ha!" kind of smile, ape-runs off with the stick to his bigger cave. He's got lots of sticks stacked in a pile, a whole hoard of them, all probably stolen. He looks back in a gloating way, rubbing this new stick against another stick. I don't know if that was primitive-style trash-talking or what, but that's what he does. And what do you know? He starts a fire. Whoosh! Little guy's stick goes up in flames. End of stick.

Big guy is now being hailed by people like Professor Basil Blahbitty-Blahblah as this wonderful, supersmart early human—the first one to discover fire.

But we know better.

We know he was really the first jerk.

CHAPTER 2
A Long History of Jerks

That big early-human stick stealer may have been the first jerk in history—or at least the first *documented* jerk—but he sure wasn't the last. History is so loaded with jerks that it would be impossible to name them all, even just in loose categories like "military jerks" or "artistic jerks" or "political jerks." It would take way, *way* too long, be very boring and involve looking up dates and facts. Also, this is a *science* project, so there is important groundbreaking research to dive into.

Just trust me on this one: jerks can be found in every era of history, in any event, big or small. War brings out a lot of jerkishness in many people, but even beyond violence, there have always been jerks in all walks of life.

For example, in ancient Greece, when everyone wore long robes, there was probably a jerk who deliberately stepped on someone else's robe when they were heading out to buy olives or invent philosophy or something. In medieval times, when knights were going out to battle in their armor, I guarantee you there was some jerk who kept clanging other knights' visors down and laughing as they fumbled with their iron mitts to get them up again. And there was probably some jerk kid in the Middle Ages who would touch less popular kids and scream about having "plague cooties."

We teach kids early about jerks and idiots. You can find them all over nursery rhymes, fairy tales and children's stories. The Big Bad Wolf in "The Three Little Pigs"? Complete jerk, obviously. I mean, even though two of those pigs weren't the sharpest tools in the shed (a wolf-proof house out of straw? Sticks? Seriously?), blowing down houses is just a jerkish thing to do. Actually, come to think of it, the Big Bad Wolf also *ate* Little Red Riding Hood, didn't he? Or am I confusing wolves? Anyway, eating people will generally launch you off the idiot-to-jerk scale into a whole different territory involving police, courts and jails. But I guarantee that everyone will agree you're also a complete jerk.

Or take "Cinderella." Hard to find bigger, more complete jerks than that wicked stepmother and her two hag daughters. Look, I'm sorry you're really ugly and crabby and have superhuge feet and all, but you think you can just lock Cinderella up and keep using her as slave labor? Uh-uh, girls.

The witch in "Hansel and Gretel"? Cree-py. Hmmm, a sinister gingerbread house in the middle of a dark forest in Nowheresville…Anyone but an idiot, or a pair of idiots, would have run away. Anyway, she's a *witch*, okay? And she apparently eats children. What is it with the eating people thing in children's books? Anyway, two important jerk clues. Most witches in children's stories are complete jerks, as are trolls, ogres and giants. And anyone with "wicked" or "evil" added to their name is a safe bet to be a total jerk.

It's also almost always safe to assume that any character who's *supposed* to be mean or evil is a complete jerk as well. Like Voldemort or Darth Vader. Complete jerks, obviously. But sometimes the superbad characters aren't supposed to be complete jerks. Sometimes they've been misunderstood, or they have a core of goodness deep down inside. Like that's believable. But think about it. In some really heavy-moral stories, the main character is a jerk who learns to become less jerkish and even sort of nice by the end of the story. Take Scrooge. He's this old, miserable guy—a complete jerk—who gets dragged around by some ghosts who show him what a jerk he's been in the past, how jerkish he is now and the jerk he might become in the future. He finally—*finally*—figures "Hey, I've been a complete jerk!" and becomes nice.

Kind of. Only, if he has to have people spell out with flashbacks and hand puppets and things how he's a complete jerk, I'm not sure I wouldn't classify him as still being an idiot.

Anyway, on a similar theme we have the Grinch, who actually steals *everything* in a whole little town (gifts, trees, furniture, food) because he hates Christmas and wants to ruin it for everybody else. "What a complete jerk!" we're supposed to think. But then the Grinch sees that his plan didn't work, because the normal, non-jerkish little Who folks held Who hands, sang and refused to let him ruin things, and so he becomes nice. In fact, his heart grows two sizes that day. Believable? Hmmm…(See Chapter 11 for a scientific look at jerks and behavior change.)

But you know what I've noticed in my scientific survey of kids' stories? That for every complete jerk, there's an idiot around. We've already mentioned Hansel and Gretel. But Goldilocks is another perfect example. Goldilocks was a total idiot. Breaking into the bears' house? Eating their porridge (*all three bowls*)? Sleeping in all of their beds? I mean, come *on*! How idiotic. In my scientific opinion, she deserved to run all the way home with three bears on her heels.

Goldilocks leads nicely into my final observation in this chapter. It's about what I call "hidden jerks."

I'm not just talking about monsters under the bed, although they might qualify. Hidden jerks are jerky characters who sort of fly under the radar, because their jerkishness is not immediately obvious.

The Cat in the Hat is a perfect example. Most people would go all "No way! Not the Cat! He gives those two pale kids some fun on that wet, wet, wet day!" So we're supposed to think. But what does he *actually* do?

He breaks into the house. Criminal behavior usually qualifies you as a jerk, as I mentioned before. But if that isn't enough for you, he brings in those two completely destructive and eerily silent little jerks, Thing One and Thing Two.

He trashes the place and annoys the kids. Anyway, sure, he cleans up his messes, but not until the mom's leg appears in one picture, like she's just coming around the corner and will be home in *seconds*, which stresses out the frantic kids completely. So really, even though the book has some pounding rhymes that you'll never get out of your head, it's all about a jerk.

The song "Rudolph the Red-Nosed Reindeer" gives us another example of hidden jerks. Eight of them, to be exact, because all of the reindeer except Rudolph were complete jerks. Ever heard the song?

Rudolph's all shy and embarrassed about his freakishly un-reindeerlike bright red nose, and *all of the other reindeer / used to laugh and call him names / They never let poor Rudolph / join in any reindeer games.* Need I say more? Sure, when he became the rock-star reindeer Santa handpicked to guide the old sleigh, they loved him, but when it really mattered they were complete and utter jerks. Bullies, even. Yet people *happily* sing this song every year, as if it's just another heartwarming holiday song.

These examples clearly show the need for some scientific research about jerks. That's where I come in (as a researcher, not a jerk).

CHAPTER 3

Organization, the Sciencey Way, Lame Definitions and the First Two of Many Scientific Illustrations

I have, in the previous two chapters, scientifically established that jerks have been around since humans began, well, being human. But as far as I can tell, no one has ever done a scientific study of what makes a jerk a jerk, identifying and studying jerkish behavior and plotting it all on very important-looking graphs and charts that should fill up some pages and earn me extra marks.

Jerks are a very large, difficult group to study. There's a lot of them, they can be found anywhere, in any situation, and they don't exactly wear *I'm A Jerk!* badges. Let's face it—the baking-soda-and-vinegar volcano (of which there will be many handed in for this assignment) would have been an easier, flashier choice for a science project.

But difficulty never stopped my scientific colleagues, like Galileo and Einstein, from discovering whatever it was they discovered. Nope, even without Google they figured out some very serious stuff.

The following sections describe how I will proceed in researching this very difficult topic.

A) Organization

Organization is the key to all serious scientific study. In this science project, I will:

1) use A) for the first things in my scientific lists, then

2) use 1) if I need to say more scientific things about A), and then

3) start with the small letters (a) for more detail about 1), then

4) use tiny roman numbers for more (i) and even more (ii) detail, but only up to maybe (iii), which is three, because it starts getting confusing with the *v*'s, so don't get attached to the roman numerals.

So, even though I've already done a very professional table of contents (which many, many other students probably forgot to add to their projects), here's a quick summary of what to expect. In this science project, I will:

1) define the terms "jerk" and "idiot," so we know what we're working with;

2) describe a highly scientific scale I have developed, which plots human behavior on a scale from "idiot" to "complete jerk";

3) research human idiocy and jerkosity, exploring key scientific areas such as:

(a) Jerks and age

(b) Jerkishness as a family trait

(c) Jerks in sports

(d) Jerks in emergency situations

(e) Jerks at school (a familiar subject)

(f) Miscellaneous jerks

(g) Jerks and behavior change

(h) Animals as jerks;

4) develop You Be the Jerk! a fun, quiz-like section where you get to put yourself in a jerk's shoes and ask yourself, "If I were a jerk here, what would I do?" (there's no grading, so no pressure);

5) come up with some concluding, very conclusive conclusions.

B) The Sciencey Way

This project will follow the **scientific method,** which, as far as I can tell, is just sort of looking at things in a sciencey way. So let's just call it "**looking at things in a sciencey way.**" So, say you want to figure something out. Like, for example, whether toddlers can be jerks (see Chapter 4).

This is your **problem.** You kind of think about it for a while and decide, "Nah, little kids can't be jerks! They're cute, mostly, and they have puny little brains.

No way can they be jerks." This is your **hypothesis**, a guess you make in a sciencey way. Then you test this idea with an **experiment**, using various **materials** (say, two toddlers and a big plastic car). You check out what happens (your **observations**) and figure out if you're right or not by making **conclusions** (which sum up what you learned and sound important and final).

For added scientific value (and, hopefully, added marks), I will use graphs, tables and charts wherever I can to illustrate my **data** (things I learned from my experiments) once I figure out how to format them on our family's ancient, lame computer. These illustrations will appear only in black and white  because, even in the interests of groundbreaking scientific research, my dad won't spend the extra money on a color cartridge for the printer. (Apparently, black and white was good enough for him when he went to school in the 1980s and had a computer the size of a dishwasher.)

Depending on the topic, some illustrations may even have to be hand-drawn, but they will still be highly scientific. Many, many scientists from the past had no computer and scribbled out their stuff by hand, and I'm very sure their teachers never lowered their grades because of it.

C) Lame Definitions

But what, you may ask, *is* a jerk? What is an idiot? What do we mean by these words? Jerks and idiots don't *look* any different from normal people, so it can be tricky. Well, let's head to the experts. The *Oxford Dictionary of English*, a very big, very heavy book, defines both words:

—> *jerk* noun, informal: *a contemptibly foolish person* (you have to get past the "sudden movement" and the "raising of a barbell above the head" definitions to get to the one we want)

—> *idiot* noun, informal: *a stupid person* (it also gets into the old definitions about people of low intelligence, which is just plain hurtful and is not the way *anybody* uses the word these days)

Now, I'm sure some very smart people wrote those definitions. You pretty much have to be smart to write dictionaries. You also have to factor in that those dictionary writers had to write a whole bunch of definitions as well, because the book is about nine thousand pages long and *heavy*.

But really? How lame can those definitions be? Even if we assume that they have to keep them short and snappy, a jerk as a "contemptibly foolish person"? An idiot as merely "a stupid person"? I think we can do better.

Recognizing jerks and idiots is instinctive. It's all about the way people act. When we say somebody is an idiot, we don't really mean they aren't intelligent. Many of the total idiots I know do very well in school. But they also do stupid and annoying things. Like, for example, the kid that repeats everything you say (he repeats everything you say!), so you tell him to shut up (*Shut up!* he mimics), so you say "Okay, now just stop it!" (*Okay, now just stop it!*). And it goes on and on until you're running away and he's running after you until you find a door between you and him that you can slam and lock.

But interestingly, while idiotic behavior can be, and usually is, highly annoying, it is rarely deliberately mean. That's jerk territory. So when we mutter "jerk" under our breath, we generally aren't thinking "You are a foolish person; therefore, I have contempt for you," like the dictionary thinks we are. What we mean when we think somebody is a jerk is that the person is *doing* something stupid or really annoying *in a deliberately stupid, annoying and mean way*. Jerks *act* like jerks. It may have started as an idiotic or jerkish idea in their brains, but it's when they start *doing* something jerkish that most of us notice.

The following diagram illustrates how this works.

Scientific Illustration #1:
The Phases of a Jerk's Behavior

1. Jerk at rest

2. Jerk getting jerkish idea

3. Jerk acting on jerkish idea

4. Recognition of jerkish behavior

You JERK!

A lot of the time, we don't really study jerkish behavior—we just recognize it at a gut level, then ignore, avoid or challenge it. So, here's an example. A few days ago, I answered a question in class and sort of stumbled over the answer. It was just a little thing. Instead of saying "double-you" for the letter *W*, I said "d*w*ubble-you." It was just a slip. Too early in the day. Whatever. Now (a) I *knew* I said it wrong (I've actually known how to pronounce that letter since I was about three years old), and my face went red and hot, and I corrected myself immediately, and (b) everyone else in class knew I said it wrong, and most of them said nothing. Most normal people just sort of think in their heads, "Oops, slipped up there." And then they let it go, because it's embarrassing, but everyone makes mistakes. That's what most normal people would do. Now, a jerk would make a huge big deal about it.

"Dwubbleyou?? DWUBBLEYOU?? You said DWUBBLEYOU!!! Ha, ha…"

This is an actual quote by a certain known jerk in my class. She could not let it go and even brought it up again at lunch. I ignored her. It was the dignified option. What can you even do about a jerk like that?

D) A Jerk by Any Other Name: A Note on Language

Often when people describe jerks, they don't say what they really mean. They use euphemisms, which are nicer, kinder words that sound better but essentially mean the same as *jerk*. Adults often do this; kids, not so much. Why this hesitation in calling a jerk a jerk? There appear to be four main reasons: being polite, being kind, being professional and being clueless.

1) Being polite

Lots of non-jerks do not publicly use the word "jerk" to describe other people. It seems impolite and somehow even illiterate, as though you couldn't think of a better word and just settled on darkly muttering, "What a jerk!" But if an adult describes someone as "a real character," "hypercompetitive," "high-maintenance," "an overachiever," "not pulling their punches," "very intense," "inflexible," "blunt" or "stressed out," they just might be delicately dancing around the word "jerk."

2) Being kind

Kind people often shy away from name-calling. That reluctance to hurt another person's feelings is part of the reason they aren't jerks themselves. I would argue that calling a jerk a jerk is more a matter of classification, but that may just be my inner scientist talking. My mom is a frustratingly kind person. Example: A new kid in my class behaves like a jerk. She's rude and disruptive and just kind of mean. But when I tell my mom, she says things like "It's hard to be the new kid," "It's early days," "It's a period of adjustment" and "Give her time." And that all might be true. But the kid might still be a jerk.

3) Being professional

Rarely, if ever, will a teacher write "This kid is a complete jerk" on a report card. Correct me if I'm wrong, but I doubt it's ever been done, even when the teacher was very, very tempted. First, it wouldn't be terribly professional. Second, report cards are read by parents, who might be kind of touchy about their child being called names by their teacher. So teachers hide behind more official-sounding teacher words when they write report cards, saying the child "does not play well with others," "is consistently disruptive in class," "makes poor choices" or "needs to work on sharing." Teachers may, when talking to parents, use words like "high-energy," "challenging," "difficult," "demanding" and

REPORT
• needs to work on sharing
• disruptive
• challenging
• high-energy
• does not play well with others
AKA → JERK

"uncooperative," or even go so far as to say the child is "a real handful" (you have to imagine the small, weary smile and the shake of the head. And the nodding of the parents). Anyway, all of these are obviously possible code words for "jerk."

4) Being clueless

Some parents must secretly know that their kids are jerks. This must be hard, because jerks are generally disliked. People pretty much want to get away from jerks. But when you've given birth to a jerk, you're stuck with them. This difficult situation explains why some parents tend to look around for reasons (however ridiculous or inapplicable) to explain away the jerkish behavior of their children. Some kids do have real medical or psychological problems and issues, obviously. But some don't. *They're just jerks.* And some parents just can't accept that their kid is a jerk. But when parents start saying that "people just don't understand" their kid, that he "needs a more supportive environment," has "got in with a bad crowd," is "going through a phase," is "deep, deep down a good person" or that he's "having some issues," they may just be looking for happier words than "jerk." And can you really blame them? They have to live with the jerk.

On a positive note, my research on my uncle Dave indicates that jerks are not locked into jerkitude for their whole lives. They can change. (See Chapter 11.)

E) A Truly Scientific Analysis

Waffly language, gut feelings, unclear definitions—the problem of jerks clearly calls out for organized, scientific study. In an attempt to make it more sciencey, I have developed a simple yet highly sophisticated tool: a scale of how people act. The next scientific illustration, Scientific Illustration #2, is an important one—so important that it's the title of the whole project. Come to think of it, it probably should have been Scientific Illustration #1, but it didn't work out that way. So much for my organization.

Scientific Illustration #2
On a Scale from Idiot to Complete Jerk:
The Jerk-O-Meter

As you can see, the scale rates a spectrum of human behavior, where 1 is normal, 3 tends into idiot territory, and past 6 you're all jerk. A complete jerk, the highest level of jerk, will get a perfect score of 10 on the Jerk-O-Meter. (I plan, at some point in the future, to develop a handheld version of the Jerk-O-Meter, similar in concept to a compass or a speedometer, that you can point at a person and observe where the red needle stops on the scale. This invaluable tool for social interaction is still, however, in the development phase.)

The scale might appear quite simple. But then again, a lot of highly important sciencey stuff starts out very simply. Like when a guy wonders why an apple falls from a tree and then comes up with the theory of gravity. *Gravity*. But though simple, my scale provides a much more precise and scientific way of measuring and comparing jerkish or idiotic behavior. Let's give it a little demo.

The guy in the car behind us who honked at my mom a *millisecond* after the light turned green this morning exhibited low-grade idiot behavior. Maybe a 3 on the scale. Normal people wait that little heartbeat before honking at the person in front of them. But, no, this guy gets all huffy and impatient the *second* the light turns. Lower-scale idiots like this are mildly annoying or irritating, but not harmful. My mom glanced in the rearview mirror, muttered "okay, okay" under her breath and then forgot about it.

If Mr. Honk had laid on the horn for longer and swerved around us, he would have jumped up the scale into the idiot-tending-to-total-idiot range (4-6 on the scale). If he'd shouted at us as he burned past us, he would have continued his climb up the scale into jerk territory (maybe a 7-8). If he'd sworn at us, cut someone else off, laid on the horn again or thrown garbage out his window, he'd probably qualify for complete jerk status, a 10 on the scale. Anything more and he'd be off the scale, heading into the darker higher numbers where the police usually become involved.

Now that we have the Jerk-O-Meter as a measuring tool, it's time to jump into the research.

CHAPTER 4
Can Young Children Be Jerks?

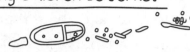

Let's be honest here—no baby is a jerk. They just can't be. Can you imagine yourself seeing a baby fussing or crying or spitting up on his mom's shoulder and saying "That kid's a real jerk!"? It's impossible. They're just little and hungry or wet and don't tend to sleep on the same schedule as the rest of us. But they don't *mean* to be annoying—I doubt if they even realize they are. So pretty much anyone who calls a baby a jerk is a jerk.

How about a toddler? They do some pretty scary stuff. They throw food. They're grabby and crabby. They have tantrums. They scream a lot. They seem to have a lot of rage. I wasn't sure if they could be jerks or not, so in the interests of science I did some research on this particular topic.

CASE STUDY #1
The Cranky Toddlers and the Big Plastic Car

Subjects: Maddie (age two, my cousin) and Nathan (age two, neighbor)

Laboratory: My auntie Anne's extremely messy family room

Experiment: My auntie Anne has one child (Maddie, a toddler) and about four thousand toys. But of all those toys, the big red plastic sit-in car is one of those premium-gold toys. What kid wouldn't want to open a big red plastic door, sit her little diaper down, slam the door and busily steer the wheel, turn the big plastic key and beep the yellow horn? None, I'm guessing. But what happens when there are two kids and one car? I observed a playdate with Maddie and her "friend" and neighbor, Nathan.

Observations: Both kids get released into the room at the same time, like a turtle race. Maddie, even though she's technically hosting this playdate, staggers across the room faster than Nathan and grabs the car. She screams "MINE!" and sort of topples through the window and eventually ends up sitting inside, grinning. Nathan sees at a glance that the car is the money toy. He starts to howl in sheer rage. He sits right down on the floor and screams until his face gets really red. Tears, snot and saliva all stream down his face. Auntie Anne rushes over and tries to reason with him. It is not even remotely successful. So she flies over to the car, gives Maddie a few quick pushes, pleads and bargains with her and eventually just wrestles her out of it so that Nathan can have a turn. Nathan stumbles over with a drooly smile and dives in, shrieking "MINE!" Maddie, predictably, goes ballistic.

To sum up, there's an undignified tussle, they have a sort of shared, collective, monster tantrum, Auntie Anne shoves the car into the garage, and things only calm down when she brings out applesauce and Goldfish crackers. And, thankfully, a wet cloth for wiping faces.

"What, you're going already?" asks Auntie Anne, noticing me putting on my shoes. "What about the research?"

"I got everything I need. Bye Auntie Anne, bye Maddie, bye Nathan!" I get gooey, applesaucy waves and "bye-byes" that spew cracker crumbs across the floor.

It's only been seven and a half minutes by my watch, but I think I have enough research. And a screaming headache.

Conclusions: Toddlers can't be jerks. They're just too young. They haven't learned not to be selfish and out of control. And they want to ride around in great little red cars. Can you blame them? Now, if Maddie and Nathan had been teenagers or adults, their behavior with the plastic car would definitely qualify them for full number-10, complete-jerk status. But they're two years old. And it's a fun car.

There appears to be an age limit for jerks, and children have to be more than two years old to properly be considered jerks.

CASE STUDY #2
Mayhem in the Mudroom

But what about kids who are older than toddlers but younger than kids in junior high (who we all know can be jerks)? Can they be jerks? In this case study, I try to pinpoint the age when jerkitude begins.

Subjects: The grade-one class at Dorothy Simpkins Elementary School

Laboratory: The mudroom

Experiment: My brother, Joe, is in grade three at this school. Every day I meet him after school and we walk home together. But in this case study, I bribed him with a cookie, told him he was my research assistant and dragged him over to observe the grade ones being dismissed for the day. What do they do? How do they behave? Can a six-year-old really be a jerk?

Observations: The bell rings. The grade ones all swarm into the mudroom, where they have to change their inside shoes for their outside shoes. It's a total scrum, and Joe and I get flattened against the wall by the human wave of six-year-olds. I can't believe how much noise these kids make. I'm regretting once again that I didn't do a quieter experiment.

Anyway, a little boy rips into the room and shoves his feet into his outdoor shoes (the kind that light up with each step you take). He heads for the door, two-hand shoving other little kids (who are bent over, putting on their shoes) out of the way and swinging his backpack. And he's also yelling "yayayayayayaaaaa!" I don't know if that's scientifically relevant, but that's what he does.

Some kids get pushed right into the metal shelves, including a little girl who bumps her head and starts to cry. She's not actually bleeding, but sometimes, at the end of a long day in grade one, a push in the back and a crack on the head can really suck. Joe and I help her find her left shoe and her teacher. The teacher looks angry and also very, very tired when she hears what the little boy (whose name is Ty) did. Ty clearly sucks up a lot of her energy. And maybe he's not even the only "high-spirited" and "challenging" child in her class of twenty-five kids.

The teacher tells me, "Ty knows better than to push his way through the mudroom. His parents and I have been working on that. And many, *many* other things."

I ask my research assistant what he thought of it all as we walk home.

"Kid's a jerk." Joe shrugs.

My brother may not be a scientist, and he may be only eight years old, but he knows a jerk when he sees one. We all do.

Conclusions: Six-year-olds can definitely be idiots and possibly even jerks. I mean, face it—when you read this case study, you immediately thought, "Little jerk!" didn't you? Okay, so maybe Ty has some hyperactivity issues or something that might explain why he acts like he does. I don't know. But he may also just be a little jerk (maybe an 8-9 on the scale).

When can a kid be scientifically classed as a jerk? I'm going to sound about ninety-five years old here, but the answer is *when they're old enough to know better.* Little Ty knew better than to shove other kids' heads into mudroom shelves. Jerk.

Even if they exhibit early jerkish behavior, young jerks may downgrade to occasional idiot behavior and then level off and become normal people. In this case study, if we followed up on young Ty (which isn't going to happen, because this report is due Thursday), we might find that his parents' and teachers' efforts to make him less jerkish have paid off. He may have become a regular, nice, normal kid. Yeah, I doubt it too.

So we're up and running. Anyone over six can be a jerk.

Scientific Illustration #3:
The Path to Complete Jerkdom

We've seen that jerks start young. But what happens when the jerkish behavior of young children is not corrected by parents, teachers, counselors or the fury of other children? Check out the following series of graphs, which show, scientifically, just how serious things can get.

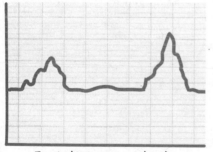

Isolated jerk activity

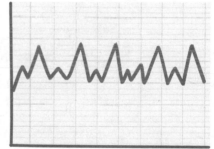

Regular jerk activity

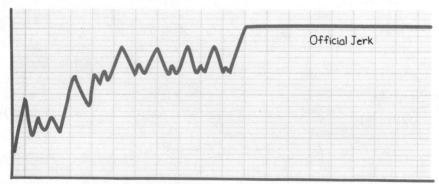

Transition to full-time, complete jerkdom

When unchecked, jerkish behavior becomes more frequent. It becomes the jerk's new normal. It can also intensify in annoyance as well as frequency. So, that kid in the seat behind you on the bus who keeps randomly kicking your seat? If nobody stops him, he might get bored with idle kicking and start in with full, rhythmic, two-feet thumping. When that becomes boring and normal, he's going to go looking for something else. And before you know it, he's launched on the path to full-time, complete jerkdom.

CHAPTER 5
Can Really, Really Old People Be Jerks?

Scientifically proving that people can be jerks as young as maybe age six got me thinking. We all know that older kids, teenagers and adults can be idiots and jerks. Nobody disputes that. But what about old people? I'm talking *really*, really old people. Is there an age at which jerkitude generally declines? Does extreme age affect a jerk's ability, energy and ingenuity? Where do really, really old people sit on the scale from idiot to complete jerk?

It seems kind of awful to research whether a great-grandmother pushing a walker is a jerk. But *can* she be one? How about that ancient toothless guy in a wheelchair? Can *he* be a jerk? In the interests of science, I took my research to another level for this groundbreaking study.

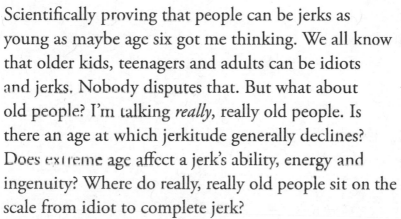

CASE STUDY #3
The Nursing Home Manly Man

Subjects: Really, really old people
Laboratory: St. Hilda's Health and Home Care Facility

Experiment: My great-grandmother lives in this very nice nursing home. All the people there have their own rooms, but there's a main dining room where they go for meals and a "social room" where they have bingo, sing-alongs, yoga, you name it. Great-Gran is eighty-nine, and she's got a busier social life than I do.

My family visits her every Sunday for about twenty hours. Once we've talked with her a bit and told her what we're doing in school, there's not a lot to do. But on this particular Sunday I had a plan. My scientific mission was to observe the behavior of all these seemingly innocent, sweet old folks. Were there jerks among them?

Observations: After we've talked a little with my great-grandmother, my dad, my brother and I go to play shuffleboard in the social room, like we always do when Mom, Grandma and Great-Gran get talking. As we played, I looked around. People playing cards. People watching TV. No cheating or gossiping or bad behavior at all. No jerks in sight. Nothing happening. I sigh and put my notepad away in my pocket.

Now, I understand that you have to be patient in scientific observation, like those people who squat in African rain forests for thirty years, interacting with the gorillas. I get that. But I'm feeling like it would take a lot longer than that to get some research done in this place. I begin to think that jerkish behavior might take a lot of energy, and that very old people might be too tired and worn out to be jerks.

Then a very old guy with a cane stumps into the room and stops. He stares at us. One of those long, unblinking stares that makes people uncomfortable. It doesn't help that he has watery, reddish eyes and a peeling, spotty head. It is an ancient, tortoise-like stare.

"THOSE CHILDREN THERE," he calls loudly to my dad, gesturing at us with his cane, "ARE THEY BOYS OR ARE THEY GIRLS?"

We all freeze.

"BOYS," my dad says cheerfully. "THEY'RE BOYS." I can tell he thinks the old guy must not be able to see very well.

The old man kind of snorts and limps in to get a closer look at us. I feel like a zoo animal. He studies us with his old, bleary eyes. He leans in so close I can smell his oldness.

"BOYS, EH? YOU'D NEVER KNOW IT!" he bellows in disgust. "LA-DI-DAH LONG HAIR... LOOK LIKE WIMMIN, THE BOTH OF THEM."

Joe and I look at each other, startled. Our hair is cool.

"WELL, YEAH, THEY MIGHT BE DUE FOR HAIRCUTS," shouts my dad, looking down and trying not to laugh. We will *never* hear the end of this one.

"HOW OLD ARE THEY?" The old guy cuts him off belligerently. Hey, pal, we're *right here*. I hate it when adults talk about you like you're not there when you're *right there*.

There is a long, loud and very tedious conversation between Dad and the old guy about our ages. And about how the old guy wasn't skipping around with girly hair playing sissy games when he was eight or thirteen. He was threshing wheat and building barns and plowing fields and fighting in wars and being a decent, short-haired, manly man.

We manage to escape from the old guy (who, incidentally, shouts after us, "IS THAT HOW YOUNG MEN *RUN* THESE DAYS??") and get around the corner before Dad bursts out laughing. It is very unprofessional. Dad is still wiping his eyes when we get back to Great-Gran, and I ask her about the old guy.

"Oh, you mean Angus," she says knowingly, nodding her head. "Cane, scabby head, SHOUTS?" Apparently, she's known him for about eighty years. She laughs when I tell her about our meeting with him.

"Well, what do you expect? Everyone knows he's a cranky old jerk. Always was."

Conclusions: The old guy was a complete jerk. Therefore, very, very old people can be jerks.

It is not mean to think of old people being jerks. We sometimes assume that all old people are nice and kind. But think about it. Old people are just *us*, only way, *way* older. The mean kid from school who steals gum from the nice people that own the corner store? He's going to be really, really old someday. A really, really old jerk.

Four generations of Murphys agreed that the old guy was a jerk. And apparently his sister, who lives there as well and who I didn't have the pleasure of meeting, is a real jerk as well. It got me thinking about how some families tend to breed jerks. It gave me the idea for my next chapter. Read on.

CHAPTER 6
Jerks in the Family

Normal families are all alike, but every jerkish family is jerkish in its own way. In this chapter, we look at whether people can be born with jerkish tendencies and then pass those on to their children and grandchildren, who in turn become jerks. It would be interesting to know if last chapter's nursing-home jerk has any children, and if so, how they turned out. Short-haired jerks, I'm guessing.

It seems pretty clear that children observing the way their jerk parents act will learn those kinds of behaviors. Normal kids learn normal things from their parents, like sharing, waiting their turn in line or chewing with their mouths shut. In a similar way, jerkish kids learn jerkish things from their jerkish parents, like cheap-shotting in hockey, bragging openly or banging on aquarium glass even though there are signs saying it hurts the fish.

But how do you explain those families who have a jerk parent (or parents) and normal, nice-ish kids? Or families where the parents are super nice but one of the kids is a jerk? It must be confusing and alarming

when jerks just appear in otherwise normal families—
normal parents, normal brother, normal sister,
then BOOM! All of a sudden you've got a jerk in
the family.

Is jerkishness really just a random occurrence, like
tornados or delicious food in the cafeteria? Or could it
be a trait passed down from generation to generation,
like brown eyes or being left-handed? There's a
scientific word for this: *heredity* (which is pronounced
"her-ED-ity" and not "here ditty," as I once thought
when I was much, much younger).

Dictionary time. The big, heavy *Oxford Dictionary
of English* says this:

→ *heredity noun: the passing on of physical or mental
characteristics genetically from one generation to another.*

So basically, what I just said but with the word
genetically thrown in there. That means, I believe,
something to do with things in your blood. I've put
the dictionary down, and I'm not opening it again.

So is jerkishness something
that can actually be passed down
from old relatives? If you trace
a family tree back far enough,
will you find ancestor jerks who
have secretly passed on their jerk
genes to unsuspecting future
generations?

The Jerk Gene

Rebecca's Confusing and Alarming Family

I was disappointed to discover that, other than my uncle Dave (see Chapter 11), both sides of my family are mostly boringly normal non-jerks. I really needed a more dysfunctional, jerk-ridden family to study, genetics-wise, for this project.

As if it was meant to be, Rebecca (not her real name), who sits in front of me in Language Arts, came in late for class last week, threw down her backpack and hissed, "My family is such a nightmare!" Nightmare family? This was just what I needed. I described my project to Rebecca, and we struck a bargain. Rebecca agreed to research her family tree with the help of her grandma, who lives with them. She was very clear about the research not going further than this project—in fact, she swore me to secrecy, so of course I agreed, and of course I'm even more interested in this family than I was before.

I agreed to collect egg cartons and gross compost materials for Rebecca's science project on seed growth, and to buy her a Slurpee sometime when a group of us go to the convenience store and it doesn't look like a date.

Subjects: Rebecca and her nonna (grandma in Italian)

Laboratory: Rebecca's house

Experiment: To save Rebecca from writing it all down, I borrowed Rebecca's family's video camera to film the interview Rebecca had with Nonna. So just remember that I had to listen to this *twice*, once live and once typing it out. All in the interests of science...

Observations: I had to heavily edit this interview (***indicates where I stopped and started), because, man, Nonna can talk. And it seems like there are about four thousand living members of Rebecca's family, many of whom Nonna either viciously hates and/or never speaks to. I am unsure about her scientific objectivity.

* * *

REBECCA (*nervously, looking at the camera*). So, Nonna, thank you for agreeing to be interviewed...

NONNA (*suspiciously*). Who's that? (*Points a finger at the camera.*)

REBECCA. I told you, Nonna. J.J. and I are interviewing you for research.

NONNA (*with heavy sarcasm*). Oh yeah, *right. Research.* You think I was born yesterday? Becca, if you think at thirteen you're going to have a boyfriend, you got another think coming! When I was thirteen...

✲ ✲ ✲

(*Nonna calms down and breezes through several generations of her family at a confusing rate, jumping from era to era, using lots of hand gestures and flipping her suspiciously black hair. She throws in bits of rumor, gossip and history. I'm not actually sure, but I think she mentions Napoleon.*)

REBECCA (*determinedly trying to bring Nonna back to the relevant points*). So *your* mother and father were nice, kind people…

NONNA. Angels, angels.

REBECCA. And Nonno (*looks at the camera*)—my grandpa, who died many years ago—*his* father…

NONNA. Was an angel. A wonderful man, Papa Silvio, so kind, so sweet…

REBECCA. But Nonno's mother, Rosa, you say was maybe not—

NONNA. A she-devil! Mama Rosa…well, the rose smells sweet, but it has thorns! You make me speak this woman's name? I remember the week before our wedding…

✲ ✲ ✲

REBECCA. So Nonno's brother, Sergio, was a jerk, and his two sisters, Marta and Sophia, were jerks.

And all of their twelve children are jerks. Is that what you're telling me? Seriously, Nonna?

NONNA (*with the satisfied air of somebody who has finally made her point*). Yes, yes. And their children's children will be too, probably.

REBECCA (*sighing*). Okay, let's move on to you and Nonno. You had three children—Frank, Isabella (my mom) and Tania.

NONNA. Angels, all of them angels. That thing with the police and Frankie? Garbage! Just garbage. The police made it up. Or they got the wrong guy. He was framed.

REBECCA (*uneasily*). Well, he did get convicted…

NONNA (*aggressively*). Who you going to believe? Your Nonna or some big-shot stranger sitting behind a desk in a courtroom?

* * *

REBECCA (*her head resting on her hand*). I know that Frankie's kids are wild, and that Tania never visits and never calls. But Mom says can you blame her? Anyway, Tania's kids are okay. Sherrie and Brianne? They're nice.

NONNA. What do I know those kids? I never see them. Never…

REBECCA (*quickly heading Nonna off from another rant*). But my mom and my dad are good people…

NONNA. Your mother is an angel. Your dad? (*She shrugs.*) He's okay.

REBECCA. And they had four children. Me, Susannah, Conor and Brayden.

NONNA. Such a stupid name, Brayden! Like the sound a donkey makes…

REBECCA. *Anyway*, it's not his name that's the problem.

NONNA. No, true, that's the least of that kid's problems. Trouble with friends, school always calling, the things we find in that backpack of his…

REBECCA (*looking wearily at the camera*). Can we stop now, J.J.?

Conclusions: I got more than I bargained for in this case study. You were right, Rebecca—that is one nightmare family you got there. And Nonna herself could be the star of some weird reality show. *My Small, Cranky, Italian Nonna!* or something like that. Anyway, in most families, people can barely remember their grandparents' last names, let alone their great-great-great grandparents' names, let alone whether or not they were jerks. So often there is a lot of guesswork involved. But Rebecca's nonna had an encyclopedic knowledge of her entire huge family, and razor-sharp memories, even if they were mostly about old feuds and grudges. So even making allowances for Nonna's lack of scientific objectivity, there seems to be evidence of a strong genetic line of jerks in Rebecca's family. Like, four generations of jerks, most of them on the non-Nonna side of the family.

For every jerk in a family, there's always a bunch of nice people that somehow have to deal with them.

Jerks and heredity could probably be a whole science project by itself. And you'd have to live about seven hundred years to really figure it all out. Gene scientists, good luck with all that. I'm fine with accepting that the science is unclear on the subject of jerks and heredity, and that it probably won't be solved by an eighth grader in one chapter of his science project. (Full marks for effort, though, wouldn't you say?)

Scientific Illustration #4:
Rebecca's Family Tree

This is as close as I could get to illustrating (some of) Rebecca's family tree. Now remember, this is a science project, not an art project. Therefore, the following stick people should just be taken as representing people, not actually looking much like them. The known jerks are the stick people with angry eyebrows and the fuming marks coming off their heads. The non-jerks are the ones smiling or looking uneasily at the jerk beside them.

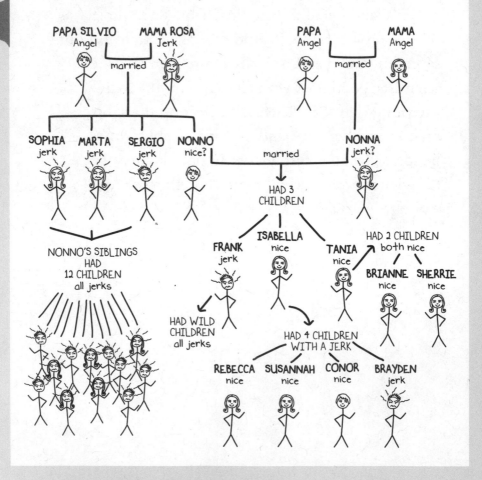

CHAPTER 7
Jerks in Sports

Like sun, water and soil for plants, sports provide the optimal environment in which jerks thrive. Many elements that contribute to prime jerkish behavior are found in sports—adrenaline, intensity, competition, pressure, physical contact and some spectators your own age. Is it any wonder jerks flourish?

For example, you're on an unexpected breakaway, skating faster than you've ever skated in your life. The ice is a blur. The crowd is screaming. You can hear your own heart pounding. There's only the goalie between you and glory. You wind up and...BOOM! Some faster-skating jerk *from your own team* swoops in, strips the puck off you and scores. This is a very recent example (last night's game) of jerks in sports, taken from my own hockey team. Faster-skating jerk, you know who you are.

In my experience, sports tend to bring out the inner jerk in many people. Is it the competition? The adrenaline? The drive to be the best? The fact that referees can't see or don't call everything? The fact that some coaches never bench faster-skating jerks for stripping the puck off fellow teammates? Whatever the reason, stories about jerks in sport could fill a whole shelf of books. If we include professional athletes, a whole library. And we'd have to come up with a new, expanded scale.

For this project, I only observed junior high school sports. Surprisingly, even where the stakes are really low, you can still manage to find some complete jerks.

Do I have to be all sensitive-supportive and mention that for every jerk there's a really great teammate/coach/fan that has a heart of gold and gives 110 percent for the team and blah, blah, blah? Obviously. If only jerks played sports, nobody else would play with them, and it'd be an all-jerks league. Sports are fun, and lots of nice non-jerks play them. But the purpose of this whole project is to seek out and analyze the bad behavior (see title of science project), so we'll focus on the jerks.

A) Players

1) Opposing Team Members

Most of the time, it's fun to imagine the other team as a bunch of jerks. It helps stir up the wanting-to-beat-them feeling. It's what any decent rivalry is based on. Sometimes, however, the other team really *is* a bunch of jerks. Take the Violet Mahoney

Junior Boys basketball team in our school's league (the Vile Baloneys, as we have cleverly nicknamed them). While my school team wanders out to warm up in mismatched shorts and ancient jerseys that reach down to our knees, the Baloneys make even warm-up a performance. They explode into the gym with blaring music and slide straight into a very slick and complicated passing drill. They all wear new school sweat suits with their names on the back. Their uniforms fit them, and they all have expensive basketball shoes. They wear matching socks. Some of them wear shooting sleeves and LeBron headbands. We heave up random shots, try to minimize our enormous armholes and fight that sinking, intimidated feeling. We despise them.

I'm not just being mean. They don't only *look* like jerks. They really *are* jerks to play against. First—and this is what sucks the most—they're really good. They beat us 107-16 last game. But I mean, come on! Right there, running up the score against a lousy team is a jerkish thing to do. It's just rubbing it in. These guys were pressing and raining in three-pointers when they were up by seventy points. Second, their coach is a jerk. He screams a lot and argues every call, and the team just follows his jerkish lead. Third, it's not just that the Baloneys are a jerk team as a whole.

Each guy on the team is an individual jerk. They shove you when the ref isn't looking, pull on your jersey, throw out a knee when they're setting a screen and are generally cheap-shot artists. Especially number five, who usually guards me and who likes to throw an elbow. Just saying.

2) Teammates

Usually, your teammates are your friends. You work together, celebrate victories, overcome defeats, build team spirit, yadda yadda yadda. But sometimes even your own teammates can be total jerks. I've already given you the example from my hockey game, but there are lots of other examples.

Take our girls volleyball team. I went to their season-opener game in the interests of science. Mostly nice girls, and they seem to get along pretty well. Except for…one girl. I'll call her X. She ruins everything for that team. X is, predictably, a jerk to the other team, firing the ball at their legs under the net when they've won the point and get to serve again, clapping when they screw up and refusing to shake hands with them. Usual jerk stuff. But she's also a huge jerk to her *own* team. The big eye roll or a loud "C'mon!" when a teammate plows a serve into the net, the shoving teammates out of the way to slam the ball over the net, the mean, hissed whispers…Yep, X is pretty much a textbook jerk. The coach, happily a non-jerk, didn't put up with her for long and benched her. She sat out the last game of the match at the far end of the bench, many empty seats away from the other players. Just a tip—that's usually the jerk zone.

B) Coaches

Okay, so I'm probably going to get in trouble on this one. But in the pursuit of scientific truth, I have to include a section on whether coaches can be jerks.

Now, adults don't generally like to criticize coaches, who are often teachers or parents who give up their weekends and evenings to hold practices and attend games and tournaments. My parents are always reminding me that coaches take time away from their own families and friends and are generally very badly paid. Actually, as I understand it, coaches at my level don't get any money for coaching. Which makes it really amazing that they show up at all, to be honest.

So most people like my parents are just very, very—almost tearfully—grateful that they don't have to be the one showing up for the six AM hockey practice or playing keep-away basketball with a gym full of hyper five-year-olds. Yes, coaches deserve a lot of praise for what they do. But I've strayed here from the focus of this project. The question is, can coaches be jerks?

I have personally never had a coach who was a jerk. There was an *assistant* coach on my hockey team (let's be honest—he was a dad who wanted the coachlike authority but none of the pressure) when I was eight who would push us onto the ice during line changes, so that we'd go sprawling on our skinny eight-year-old legs. He claimed it was just to "start us off." He was an idiot (but probably only a 3 or 4 on the scale), but otherwise, I've been pretty lucky.

My brother Joe? Not so lucky. He had a soccer coach a couple of summers ago who was unbelievable. I'm talking off the Jerk-O-Meter, ranting, cheating, hypercompetitive lunatic jerk. Coaching six-year-olds! Here's a tip. If a coach ever SCREAMS at a six-year-old, he's a complete jerk. This guy would scribble out complicated "plays" on clipboards and then yell at the team to "run the offense! RUN. THE. OFFENSE!" Sir, you have only two players willing to even get on the field, because the others have either quit, are crying or are hiding behind their parents' legs.

Incidentally, this coach's daughter was a total cheater too, once scoring a goal by *throwing* the ball into the opposing net while the ref wasn't looking. The coach saw it, but whooped and hand-slapped as if it was a genuine, non-cheater goal. Which raises once again the important scientific question of whether jerkishness is a trait passed down from parent to child, from generation to generation. (See Chapter 6.) Anyway, long story short, the team folded and the league had to call in counselors mid-season. Joe hasn't touched a soccer ball since.

C) Fans

Whether they are friends or family members, fans are a huge part of any game. That's why playing at home gives a team a 27 percent increased chance of winning. *Twenty-seven percent!* Okay, I made up that percentage, but I'm sure it's somewhere around that. Ever hear of home-field advantage? It's not actually the *field* that's the advantage. I used to think that too. Turns out it's mostly the fans.

Speaking from a junior high sports perspective, most of our fans are parents who clap politely and yell "good try" even when it wasn't. Sometimes groups of friends come out and act stupid, but in a fun way. Sometimes things turn ugly. And here we have to talk about Mrs. Malinowski. I can use her real name because the Malinowskis moved away last year. Far, far away.

CASE STUDY #5
The Fan Who Cost Us the Game

Subject: Mrs. Malinowski, Stuart's mom

Laboratory: Our school gym, our final basketball game last season (this case study is from memory, but it was a very, very memorable game)

Experiment: Despite Stuart Malinowski's hiding the fact that he made the junior basketball team and deliberately shredding all paperwork about game times and tournament schedules, his mom somehow managed to show up for everything. She seemed like a normal mom if you saw her driving their van or chatting with a teacher, but man, get her in a gym or an arena and she was a complete monster. I knew this from early hockey days when she would bang her feet on the bleachers so loudly that you could feel the vibrations through your skates on the ice. Also, she used an air horn, which didn't do anything other than make kids on both teams startle, skitter and fall. Anyway, this case study details (again, from memory, which might be seen by some people as impressive) an episode from our final game of the season. Our record to this point was 0-12. This was our big chance, and we were desperate to end the season with a win in front of our own few loyal and long-suffering fans.

Observations: We're playing the second-worst team in the league, and the game is tied 46-46. There are eight seconds on the clock, and everyone is very tense as we come out of a time-out— everyone including Mrs. Malinowski, who has been growling and yelling at the ref the whole game and annoying and embarrassing everyone around her so that she is sitting alone in a little empty clearing on the bleachers. The other, normal parents end up sitting in another area of the gym in order to lower their blood pressure and watch the game in peace. So our team inbounds the ball, a guy on the other team tries to steal it, and things explode.

MRS. MALINOWSKI (*screaming*). FOUL!!! YOU COMPLETE MORON! ARE YOU ACTUALLY A *REFEREE*? WHEN ARE YOU EVER GOING TO *CALL* SOMETHING?

REF (*quietly, looking grim and obviously at the end of his patience*). Coach, control your fans.

(*Coach looks uneasily at the bleachers and wipes a hand across his face. He too has been rattled by Mrs. Malinowski's game-long screaming. He clears his throat.*)

COACH. Okay, everyone calm down.

(*As though all the fans are part of the problem. This is a classic, nonconfrontational way of dealing with jerks.*)

MRS. MALINOWSKI (*quieter*). I'll calm down when this joker learns how to use his whistle…

(*The other team gets to inbound the ball now, with six seconds left. As they approach our basket, Stuart Malinowski, who's tall but hopeless, sort of swipes at the ball, gets his giraffe legs all tangled and crumples.*)

MRS. MALINOWSKI (*on her feet*). OFFENSIVE FOUL! OFFENSIVE FOUL! DO YOU ACTUALLY HAVE TO SEE *BLOOD* BEFORE YOU'LL BLOW THAT WHISTLE??

REF (*turning immediately to our coach*). Technical foul, blue team. And that fan is out of the gym. Now.

Yes, we get a foul as a team because one player's parent is a jerk. How fair is that? Their team gets their best shooter to take the foul shot, and despite Mrs. Malinowski yelling "MISS, MISS, MISS!" over her shoulder as another parent pulls her out of the gym, he makes the shot. We lose the game. Thanks a bunch, Mrs. Malinowski.

Conclusions: Obviously, fans can be jerks who ruin the fun of a game and can even lose a game for you.

Poor Stuart stammered out an apology to the whole team, but nobody blamed him. He couldn't do anything about his mom. He was a good guy. He couldn't help it that his mom was a complete jerk.

And you can't judge a kid by his jerk parents.
(See Chapter 6.)

D) Referees

As the last case study demonstrates, being a referee is not always an enjoyable job. In fact, I don't know why anybody becomes a ref. Everybody complains about the ref and how the game was reffed. The losing team blames its lousy game on the refs. You get screamed at by people like Mrs. Malinowski. It just seems like a ton of stress, even though, unlike coaches, refs get paid.

Most refs seem to deal quite well with being disliked and treated with suspicion. These are the refs who try to call games fairly, according to the rules, and who manage to keep a cone of ref dignity around them. A player comes at you to complain? The good refs look away and put up their hand, like "talk to my hand, you whiner." A coach screams at you from the bench? Dignified ref calmly makes a hand signal to throw him out of the game. Refs are big on the hand signals. So instead of roaring, "Hey! Jerk coach! Shut up! You've been screaming all game long and I've had it!" the ref just calmly makes a T sign, one hand on top of the other. Problem solved.

Calmness, fairness, consistency and cool, secret hand signals. That's reffing.

But every once in a while you come across a ref who hasn't read the same manual as the others. One of our basketball refs this year clearly didn't understand the ref code. And he seemed to be having a really bad day—or else his hair-trigger temper was just normal for him.

So here's a sample of how the game went (it's not a big enough deal to turn it into a scientific case study).

REF. Out of bounds! Yellow ball!

ONE OF OUR FANS (*calling out normally, not aggressively*). What? He wasn't out of bounds!

REF (*turning menacingly to the crowd, his face red*). WHO SAID THAT? WHO? ARE YOU KIDDING??? HIS FOOT WAS RIGHT ON THE LINE!

(*The game continues uneasily.*)

REF. FOUL, number eight! Push!

(*We all look around, confused, because number eight is me, and I'm alone on the other side of the key from the action, in my avoid-the-action spot. Did he mean number eighteen? Twenty-eight?*)

ME. Um, sir, I think there's been a mistake. I was way over there on the other side of the key…

REF. NO BACK CHAT, NUMBER EIGHT, OR I'LL THROW YOU OUT OF THE GAME!

We played very quiet, don't-upset-the-ref basketball that game.

Ignore. My dad left his coffee cup here.

CHAPTER 8
Jerks in a Crisis

Crisis situations—like fires, accidents and medical emergencies—are those rare events that happen quickly and demand lightning-fast responses. These situations cause teachers and principals to totally freak out and make parents even more anxious and worried than they usually are. Those same events exhilarate junior high students, liven up boring day-to-day routines, spark way more interesting texting and often lead to classes getting canceled.

Scientifically speaking, crisis situations provide the most pure setting in which to observe human behavior, as the combination of stress, fear and action tends to turn some people into running, screaming, wild-eyed animals. These are the situations in which heroes step up. They are also the situations in which jerks are revealed.

Amazingly, even though crisis situations are very rare—months and even years can go by without one—there are two video case studies in this section. Two! They both happened in the same week, and before anyone gets any ideas, I didn't cause either of them. Both of these events were unplanned, obviously. Our teacher knew there would be a fire drill sometime that day, and she gave Spin, my research assistant, a heads-up so that he could have his camera ready when the alarm went off. But in the second case study, it was cool-headed, scientific, quick thinking that enabled the episode to be captured on camera.

CASE STUDY #6
The Fire-Drill Drama

Subjects: The students in 8E

Laboratory: Their classroom

Experiment: This case study examines a grade-eight class's response to a routine fire drill. We've been practicing what to do in the event of a fire since kindergarten—that's every year for nine long years. Everyone knows the drill by now—single file, walk quickly but no running, last person shuts the door, gather on the lawn to get counted, joke around excitedly until they turn off that deafening alarm. You might think fire drills have become so routine and automatic that they aren't really even technically crisis situations anymore. Wrong. This case study shows how a jerk exploits the opportunity of a routine fire drill to create a crisis for his own jerkish purposes.

8

My friend Spin volunteered to help research this topic because:

1) the "Can Animals Be Jerks?" topic (his first choice) was already done;

2) he has a new cell phone with a good video cam (we call it the Spin-cam);

3) we have a nice teacher, who agreed, in the interests of science, to let Spin film the fire drill.

Even though it was incredibly time-consuming, I have typed out everything that happens in these short video segments, because meticulous, accurate documentation of detail is so very important to any scientific study. And also because Spin can't figure out how to download the videos so I can provide a link instead of writing it all out.

Observations: (*Spin's head appears. He is apparently in the boys' locker room.*)

SPIN. *Finally* found a quiet spot to practice using the Spin-cam…seems to be working. (*Useless shot panning across some chipped, dented lockers.*) Okay, operational. (*Back to Spin's head.*) Well, Luke Spinelli here. I just thought since I wouldn't get a chance to do a formal intro to this case study, I'd say a few words now. Our teacher knows that I'm helping J.J. do research on crisis situations, and, sadly, this fire drill appears to be the closest we're getting to a real crisis.

A fire drill is sort of a fake crisis, but you never know—
there might be some excitement. In grade five, Dwayne
Hepner freaked out all the teachers by going missing
during the drill. They eventually found him wolfing
down desserts from other kids' lunches. Anyway, here's
hoping this drill is, uh (*looks down at words written on
his hand*), illuminating and highly groundbreaking,
scientifically speaking. Is that right, J.J.?

ME. Shut up, Spin, and get to the video.

(*The video stops, then pops to life again, showing Mrs.
Driscoll at the front of Spin's class.*)

MRS. DRISCOLL. So, class, I think we're done with
the analysis of this nov—

ALARM. AAAAAAAAAAAAAAAAAAAAAAAAAAAA
AAAAAAAAAA!

(*You have to imagine that this goes on for the entire
video. Why are all these case studies so loud?*)

SPIN (*with Spin-cam focused uselessly on the
intercom*). Here we go! Man, that's loud…I can feel it
in my chest!

(*The camera scans the class. Everyone is standing
up, scrambling to grab their cell phones and iPods
even though nine years of drills have told them to leave
everything behind. They start to shuffle over to the door.
Contrary to training, they are moving neither quickly nor
in an orderly fashion.*)

MRS. DRISCOLL (*irritably, shouting above the alarm*).
A LINE! FORM A LINE!

(*She swings her arms back and forth like an air-traffic controller. The Spin-cam scans the lineup and stops at the end, where two girls are huddled together, looking nervous and covering their ears. Shay, a legendary jerk, slips into line behind them. He looks like he's enjoying himself. Spin zooms in.*)

SHAY (*loudly, tapping on Maddie's shoulder*). Are we *sure* this is just a drill and not a real fire??

MADDIE (*nervously*). Of course it's just a drill. It's always a drill.

SHAY. I heard it was a *real fire*…WAIT. (*He stops and sniffs.*) Do you smell that? (*His eyes widen fake fearfully.*) I smell smoke!

MADDIE (*panicking*). What?? Smoke?? (*She grabs Kaylie's arm.*) Do you smell smoke? Is there smoke? I think I smell smoke!

(*Shay grins.*)

KAYLIE. Smoke! Omigod, I smell it too!! We gotta get out of here.

(*They start pushing the kids who are already lined up. Those kids shove back. As Mrs. Driscoll opens the door, some of the kids stumble and fall, and some bolt into the hall. Spin catches one last glimpse of Shay, yelling into Maddie's ear.*)

SHAY. Hurry, HURRY! I just saw *flames* outside the classroom window!!

MADDIE AND KAYLIE. Aaaaaaaaahh!

(*Shay turns, notices Spin filming and knocks the phone out of Spin's hands. The aptly named Spin-cam gets a whirling shot of desks and floor. The video ends abruptly.*)

* * *

(*The video starts again later in the locker room, showing a gross overflowing garbage can.*)

SPIN. Oh, good, Spin-cam still works. Skidded right across the room there. (*Spin's face appears.*) Well, *that* was more interesting than I thought it would be. Pretty impressive that I caught that jerk Sha—I mean, I hope this case study gave you enough, um (*looks down at the writing on his hand*), raw data to draw numerous important and highly scientific conclusions, J.J. (*Grins.*) Research Assistant Spin and the Spin-cam, signing off.

Conclusions: Shay is a skillful jerk. During a fire drill, what kid hasn't wondered uneasily if it's a real fire? Notice how Shay used this niggling fear, fuelled it and let it spread like, well, like wildfire? He also managed to avoid any blame for the panic, while Maddie and Kaylie got detention for pushing the other kids. Completely diabolical. Shay's a complete jerk most of the time, so I might even go so far as to make a scientific finding that crisis situations intensify a jerk's natural jerkishness.

Maddie and Kaylie weren't jerks, even though they were technically the ones to push the other kids. While pushing is obviously not optimal fire-drill etiquette, they were acting out of fear rather than jerkishness. They were just nervous about the situation, rattled by that crazy-loud siren and freaked out by Shay's jerkish little mind games. At most, they were idiots to listen to Shay at all, let alone believe him.

CASE STUDY #7
Sanjiv's Hideous Injury

This case study was a last-minute addition to this science project, but it's just too good to leave out. I mean, there aren't so many genuine crises that you can afford to let one go to waste. And good old Spin managed to capture most of it on the Spin-cam.

Subjects: Grade-eight students
Laboratory: The field, lunchtime
Experiment: Here's the setup. It was *finally* warm enough to go outside, so we were all out in the field. We were laughing and talking and goofing around

when disaster struck. Alex, the biggest guy in grade eight, jumped to catch a football thrown by Spence (second-biggest guy in grade eight), landed in a sprawl and cannoned into my friend Sanjiv (who's probably the smallest guy in grade eight). Sanjiv went flying. It happened in a split second. One minute Sanjiv was up, the next he was down. And *man,* was he ever down. He couldn't stand up, he was grimacing in pain, and he was clutching his leg, which was bent in a spot where a normal leg doesn't bend. It was as if there was a whole new joint between Sanjiv's knee and his ankle. Nowhere to hide *that* injury in skinny jeans, let me tell you. Spin, who was in another group a little way off, heard gasps of panic, sensed something going on, flicked on the Spin-cam and ran over.

Observations: (*Everyone has their lips sucked into their teeth or their hands over their mouths. I'm not sure why people do that when they see an injury, but they do. Sanjiv's leg really is a gruesome sight. We're all pretty much used to legs bending in the usual places.*)

ALEX (*glancing over his shoulder*). What? I hardly touched him! Just get *up,* Sanjiv.

SPENCE (*walking over*). Yeah, man *up, Sanjiv.* Whoa! (*He sees Sanjiv's leg and gets Alex's attention by smacking him on the shoulder and pointing. They stare.*)

ALEX (*looking very pale and queasy*). It's not my fault. I was just catching the ball! It was Sanjiv! He was in my way. If he hadn't gotten in my way…

SPIN (*running over*). I'm videoing here, so this better be goo—oh, jeez! Sanjiv, you okay? (*The camera rolls up to Sanjiv's face, then down to his weirdly, scarily bent leg and stays there, jittering.*)

WESTON (*shrilly*). Of course he's not okay! Look at him! Look at his *leg*!

ALEX. *He* was the one who—

SANJIV (*wincing in pain, eyes tightly closed*). I think…it might be…broken…

ME. I'm no doctor, Sanjiv, but that sucker's broken for *sure*, so—

ALEX. It's not my fault, okay? It's not my—

ANGELA. I'll go tell a teacher! (*Runs off.*)

(*Just when we don't need it, rain starts to pelt down.*)

WESTON (*shrilly*). What should we do? We gotta *do* something! We can't just leave him *lying* here in the rain! (*There is silence as the group stares uneasily at The Leg.*)

ME (*fighting to stay calm*). Okay, okay. Let's think. Who's big? Who can carry him? Alex? Spence? C'mon, guys!

(*The two bodybuilders of the class, who are always flexing their pecs and chugging protein shakes, stagger backward, holding their hands palm out as if warding off a vampire.*)

ALEX. No way, man! You *seen* that leg? (*Sprints off, followed by Spence.*)

EDIE (*calmly*). You guys are idiots. We can't move him. I'll call nine-one-one while we wait for a teacher.

ME (*visibly relieved and shaking*). Yeah, yeah, that's right! We *can't* move him! We shouldn't! Nine-one-one…

(*The camera is still on, but Spin isn't aiming it at Sanjiv anymore. All it's recording is grass and shoes. Fortunately, the audio picks up everything.*)

SPIN. Yeah, we just gotta wait for an ambulance, make him comfortable. (*Shouts down at Sanjiv, lying on the rocky ground in the driving rain.*) You comfortable, Sanjiv? You okay?

CHAN. Does he *look* comfortable, Spin? Turn that thing off. Look, everybody give me your hoodies. (*The camera clicks off. Everyone peels off their coats, and Chan stuffs one under Sanjiv's head and spreads the rest on top of him. We wait, shivering, for people who really know what the heck to do in a crisis.*)

Conclusions: So, obviously, not everyone acts perfectly in a crisis. Not muscle guys, not even scientists. There are some interesting conclusions to be drawn from this case study.

1) To be a jerk, you usually have to do something deliberately jerkish. But sometimes, not doing anything makes you a jerk as well. While Alex didn't deliberately cause Sanjiv to go flying (it was clearly an accident), he still acted like a jerk because:

> (a) he was more concerned with telling everyone it wasn't his fault than apologizing or helping Sanjiv;
>
> (b) he actually *blamed* Sanjiv for causing the accident in the first place (which was a total lie); and
>
> (c) given the chance to help Sanjiv (okay, I admit that carrying him into the school was a stupid idea, but that's beside the point), he didn't.

I would appreciate it if this scientific conclusion remained confidential. Both Alex and Spence, huge and surly at the best of times, are more belligerent than ever since the whole school saw them run away during this case study. We are all quietly enjoying their predicament, but the situation remains delicate.

2) Sometimes, being in a crowd makes you act more stupid (though not necessarily more jerkish) than you would normally act. For example, we've all seen the shows, we all know you don't move people who are hideously injured. But it's completely

different when it's real, when it's your friend lying there.

We all stood there, kind of numb and paralyzed, waiting for somebody else to do something. Angela finally started the rescue ball rolling when she ran for help. While only Alex was really a jerk in this situation, lots of people didn't act perfectly. I myself regret my lack of scientific objectivity. But maybe that's the conclusion—in a crisis, whether there are jerks around or not, leave the crisis management to the professionals.

***A note on informed consent of participants to these scientific studies**: Sanjiv agreed to let me use this video clip in my project—I mean, after his operation, when his leg was fixed with hardware-store-sounding stuff like "screws and plates." It was only right to get his permission and possibly only legal. He actually seemed quite proud of his leg being involved in a groundbreaking scientific study.

I also got Maddie's and Kaylie's consent for the previous case study. (In fact, they're still so mad at Shay that they want me to turn Spin's video over to the teacher as evidence that it was all Shay's fault.) And as for Shay, I'm taking "get lost, freak" as acknowledgment, which is sort of like consent.

CHAPTER 9
Jerks at School

Although the events in the last chapter technically happened at school, they were unusual, dramatic events. Most of the time, school is *way* less exciting, following a predictable, often grinding routine of same old, same old, day after day. The focus of this chapter is on the more day-to-day, routine opportunities for jerks to be jerks.

A) Students

It might appear that this topic isn't even very challenging, because everyone knows that kids at school can be idiots and jerks. It's totally obvious, even to non-sciencey types. So in this section I decided to do something different.
I looked at *patterns* of jerkish behavior. Does jerkish behavior even follow a pattern? Does it peak at certain times of the day? Can one jerk acting jerkish cause other people to act like jerks? Prepare yourself for some amazingly impressive graphs.

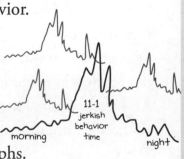

morning   11-1
jerkish
behavior
time   night

The Arc of Jerkish Behavior

Subjects: No real names will be used in this example, to prevent my having unpleasant experiences if this report ever gets seen by somebody other than my teacher. So, say there's this known jerk at school who has blond, not black, hair. He's also got green, not brown, eyes. This known jerk is really, really good at math and is not on any sports teams. We'll call him Kevin. Any resemblance to any real person or persons in this case study is purely accidental.

Laboratory: Math class

Experiment: Kevin is a guy who goes looking for ways to be a jerk. There is no doubt that he *is* a jerk (ask absolutely anyone at my school). So in this experiment, I decided to observe not *whether* Kevin is a jerk, but *how* he is a jerk.

Observations: Kevin hates math class because… because he's so good at it. Yeah, because he's so *good* at math. He's bored. He looks around. He crumples paper and fires it at a nearby girl's head. She ignores him, so he looks around some more. The student in front of him is working. Kevin grabs his ruler and pushes the other kid's arm so that his pencil goes skidding across the page. Again and again Kevin does this, despite the kid becoming more and more upset. The substitute teacher looks up from whatever she's doing (reading a novel? texting?) and tells him to "stop it, mister."

Kevin then waits until the substitute teacher figures she should probably at least pretend to teach something, just in case another teacher walks by. When the kid next to him is trying to answer a question, Kevin whispers random numbers, just to confuse him. "Four, nineteen, seventy…[giggle, giggle]…six." The guy's a total idiot as well as a complete jerk. Anyway, when the teacher's back is turned to the class, Kevin quietly rushes to the window. He slips out and slides down a nearby tree to the ground floor.

When we all look out, Kevin is across the field at the elementary-school playground, flinging the swings so hard that they go around and around the bar until they're too short for the little kids who are looking forward to using them when recess rolls around. When he's finished wrecking the swings, he wanders around the field aimlessly. Later that afternoon, the school custodian has to bring a ladder out to fix the swings.

I could go on. Kevin could probably fill up this project. But I won't, because it's illustration time.

Scientific Illustration #5: Bell Graph of a Jerk

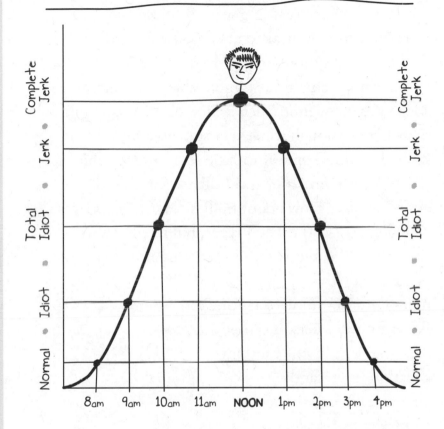

This bell graph, which is a kind of graph often used for illustrating important scientific things (and not only bells), shows how a school jerk's jerkitude builds steadily, then peaks. Apparently, jerks have to wake up fully to really embrace their inner jerk and sustain a period of busy jerkishness. Then boredom or exhaustion sets in, and jerkitude diminishes. Jerkish behavior clearly takes a lot of energy.

Conclusions: Kevin became a jerk gradually during this math class. He sort of slid up the scale from idiot to jerk, peaked at complete jerk, then slid down as he got more tired or bored.

Jerkosity seems almost impossible to sustain over a long period of time (such as, for example, a whole school day), though some very special jerks (such as some celebrities) appear to have set records in this area.

***A note on jerks and bullies:** Are complete jerks always bullies? How about bullies? Are they *always* complete jerks? The way I see it, bullies are always complete jerks, but complete jerks are not always bullies. Now that's getting pretty philosophical, but it's scientific too. For example, a person can be a complete jerk in one random situation (say, standing up and deliberately rocking a canoe at camp when all the other kids are terrified of falling into the leech-infested water). But unless this kid keeps targeting certain other kids over a longish period of time, he doesn't quite enter bully territory. Bullies, the super-jerks of the world, are a topic all on their own. But that's a science project for another day.

CASE STUDY #9
Graphing Solo Jerks and Groups of Jerks

Subjects: The popular kids in grade eight

Laboratory: The lunchroom

Experiment: I secretly studied this group over a series of lunchtimes, my notebook hidden under the table. I didn't actually need to be very secret, because this group never notices me, and they expect people to watch them. What's the point of being popular if nobody's looking?

Observations: Unlike Kevin, the jerk from Case Study #8, the popular kids in grade eight aren't all obvious jerks. In fact, many of them behave quite normally, if maybe annoyingly. But I sacrifice four lunchtimes to science and observe many jerkish events, best displayed on another amazingly scientific graph, this time one of those very official spiky, heartbeaty-looking graphs.

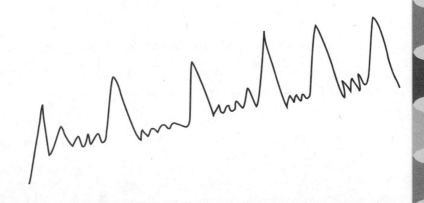

Scientific Illustration #6:
Graphing How Jerks Respond to Jerkish Events

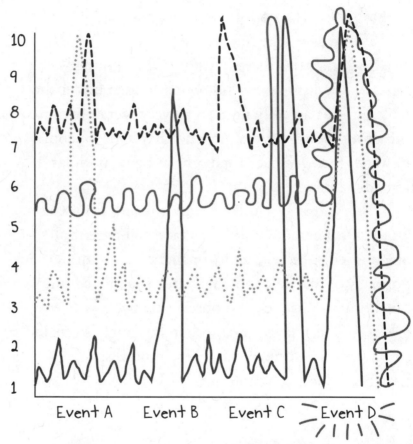

This graph took a lot of time. While it looks complicated and very impressive, it is actually pretty simple. The different lines on the graph represent different people. I only picked four, but believe me, I could have added more. There's Miss Dot, Miss Dash, Mr. Solid and Mr. Wavy. This may sound like the intro to a lame preschool TV show, but trust me, it gets better.

Note that each line spikes on the jerk scale at certain times, shown by the letters A, B, C and D. These are jerkish events. Here are some examples.

→ **Jerkish Event A:** A non-popular girl comes into the lunchroom. She has a very unfortunate, drastic new haircut. One side is *way* shorter than the other (like, scalp-showingly short) and the remaining hair is dyed a purple shade not found in nature. Most people just sort of ignore the bad hair and eat their lunches. We've all made some mistakes in the hair department. I won't get into a brutal bowl cut I once got at a cut-rate "salon" my mom dragged me to. Anyway, non-popular girl's friends make room for her at their table, being careful not to stare too long at the purple mess. But two girls from the popular group burst out laughing, cover their mouths and whisper loudly, "OMG, bad hair day has a *whole new meaning*!" Note on the graph that Dot and Dash (both girls with perfect hair) really spike to total jerks at this event.

→ **Jerkish Event B:** I stumble on a fold in the carpet as I walk past the popular group. "Hey, walk much?" calls Solid (a jerkish guy who I can't stand), and he sort of mimics my stumble, making it seem way bigger and way more embarrassing than it really was. The whole group laughs. Okay, so maybe this isn't a hugely jerkish thing, but it was mean, it happened to me, and I happened to be walking near a certain girl who also happened to look up…Anyway, that's B.

——→ **Jerkish Event C**: So Solid and Wavy think they're extremely cool because they're on the senior basketball team. Solid carries around a basketball all the time so nobody forgets that fact. So they start passing it around in the lunchroom, keeping it away from any non-popular kids who try to get in the game, "shooting" over top of people, etc. The ball sails wide and sends another kid's burger flying into the giant dustballs in the corner, and all they do is yell, "C'mon, BALL! Pass it!" So this kid gets:

- No lunch
- No apology
- *Yelled* at

Add it all up, and you get two complete jerks (note how the solid and wavy lines spike on the jerk scale on the graph).

——→ **Jerkish Event D**: A girl approaches the popular group. She used to be in the popular group, but for some mysterious, much-gossiped-over popular-group reason she got kicked out. She says something I can't hear, but in a friendly way—you know, with a smile. The popular kids look at her unsmilingly, then look away. They totally ignore the girl, who is still standing there. Then one of them clearly suggests leaving, and they get up and leave the other girl standing there. Jerks. This may not sound like very much, but trust me, in junior high, it really is. All the jerks (Dot, Dash, Solid and Wavy) spike to complete jerks during this event.

This last jerkish event might also be depicted by a cool diagram (a diagram within the explanation of a graph! Does this guy ever stop?). Ever hear of Venn diagrams? They're circles, mostly, developed by somebody named Venn, I guess. Anyway, all the circles sort of overlap in one shaded, overlapping part. It looks like the kind of doodling kids do on their binders in a boring class, but I'm told it's more significant.

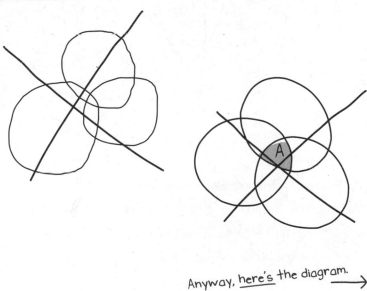

Anyway, here's the diagram. →

Scientific Illustration #7:
Quadrants of Jerkish Behavior

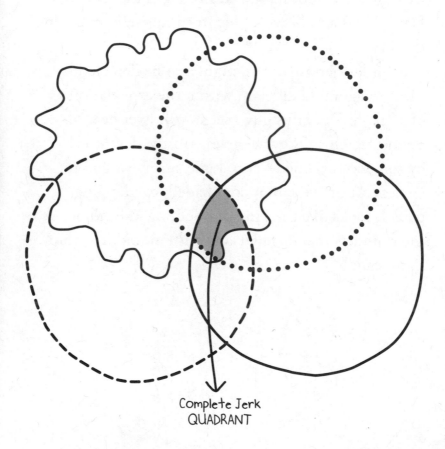

Complete Jerk
QUADRANT

In this illustration, all the circles represent the jerkish
behavior of the popular crowd. The overlap area shows
a highly concentrated and coordinated area of jerkish activity
(like when the group all dissed the formerly popular girl).
We will label that area Complete Jerk Quadrant because
quadrant is such a cool science word.

Conclusions: A highly detailed, multi-lined graph, a diagram and four lunch periods of research: I've spent way too much time on this case study already. And what did it prove? Interestingly, it didn't only show what everyone already knows—that these four jerks are indeed jerks (although it's always nice to have that documented officially). It also demonstrated two very important general conclusions about jerks:

1) Leaving aside the really hard cases for the counselors and psychologists, jerks rarely demonstrate their jerkitude all the time. Much of the time, jerks pretend to be normal people. Like that fools anybody. But at key times—during jerkish events, episodes or opportunities—their true natures are revealed and the jerkitude spikes.

2) When we think of jerks, we often think of individual jerks acting annoying all on their own. But the really groundbreaking part of this case study shows several jerks working together in a group to create a massive jerkish event. Sort of like animals that hunt in a pack, only jerkier.

B) Teachers and Principals
1) Teachers

We come to the tricky part of the project. You might think that talking about whether teachers can be jerks in a project that will be graded by a *teacher* might result in some kind of a conflict. You know, be a little awkward. Absolutely not. We're all objective professionals here. No names will be used. All scenarios described will remain anonymous and highly scientific.

Anyway, much like coaches, many, many teachers are wonderful people. They inspire kids to learn and devote themselves to education. Especially my favorite teacher, who is kind and caring and really appreciates a good science project when she reads one.

But let's face it. Regular people can be idiots and jerks, so teachers are likely no exception.

For this chapter, I:

    (a) held a scientific focus group (my friends) to

        (i) develop a list of the kinds of jerkish behavior they had personally witnessed among their teachers (this list has been edited—heavily edited) and

        ii) rate the behaviors on the Jerk-O-Meter from 1 to 10 (1 being normal, 10 being complete jerk);

    (b) paid the focus group in fruit gummies and assorted snacks; and

    (c) came up with the project's first scientific table to display the results.

Scientific Illustration #8:
Rating Annoying Teacher Behavior

Teachers have, in the last fifty or so years, been prevented by various laws from being the kind of jerks your parents' teachers might have been. Most of them don't scream a lot anymore or try to deliberately humiliate kids. Even so, there still seems to be a lot of room for idiocy and jerkishness in the classroom.

TEACHER BEHAVIOR	RATING	REASON
Deliberately calling on a kid who's staring down at his desk and not making eye contact at all.	3	Staring down at your desk, the universal kid symbol for "please leave me alone/I don't know/I don't want to answer" should be respected.
Making the "last one in" do ten push-ups in gym class.	4	Teachers never factor in distance here. It's always assumed that you're just slacking, rather than, say, playing goal at the far end of the field like I was last gym class.
Making everyone do laps even if only one person misbehaves.	7	Running senseless laps is even more stupid than push-ups. This punishment is unfair and tends to lead to a lot of group anger against the misbehaver. Which, come to think of it, might be the point.

TEACHER BEHAVIOR	RATING	REASON
Thinking that running laps around the school is an appropriate, character-building punishment.	5	Laps have nothing to do with character. This is entering total idiot territory.
Forcing us to do an entire "dance" unit and getting mad when junior high boys (and most of the girls) both dread it and suck at it.	6	You tell me when we'll ever really need to "Bollywood dance" and I'll smile through it.
Bragging about the awards or championships they won when they were our age (twenty or thirty years ago).	6-7	Bragging on its own is just idiotic. If accompanied by pelting volleyball spike-serves at us, it moves into jerkdom. There is no place on the scale to show that this is also pathetic.
Making the entire class stay after school because one kid threw a snowball.	7	One kid. One snowball. Do the math.
Assigning extra homework in a snitty voice because of the snowball incident.	$\sqrt{8}$	Bonus move up the scale for taking the whole incident up a notch. What does homework have to do with snowballs, anyway?

TEACHER BEHAVIOR	RATING	REASON
Using student slang (e.g., Teacher: "That is so fresh! YOLO!")	3	Believe me, this does not help kids relate to the teacher at all. It just gives them material for LOL-ing at them behind their backs.
Using heavy sarcasm (e.g., Teacher: "Yeah, you guys are really going to be ready for high school.")	7	We understand, so you don't have to be mean about it. And the sarcasm isn't preparing us for anything either.
Playing their lame music in class and getting mad when kids complain about its lameness.	3	This is low-grade idiot behavior, but we're a captive audience, and that makes us angry.
Using obvious bluffs (e.g., Teacher: "If this class doesn't settle down, you will all fail health class!")	5	Nobody fails Health.
Being either way too uncomfortable or way too comfortable with the body stuff in Health.	2-4	The rating will depend on our degree of comfort or discomfort. It's a fine line, that's for sure.
Dancing at school dances (or dancing at school ever).	?	Not really on the scale, but the focus group agreed that nobody wants to see this.

2) Principals

Our principal has often mentioned how the word *principal* includes the word *pal*. Yep, just think of him or her as a good buddy who knows all your marks, talks with your teachers and parents and could expel you.

I found our principal to be an elusive and difficult subject for research. He tended to be:

    (a) in very boring meetings;

    (b) in his office on the phone, behind that scary secretary;

    (c) dealing with more important things than my science project (like finding the jerk who swung the elementary swings around and around); and

    (d) unwilling to answer questions about why principals might be jerks or idiots.

Teachers are no help here. Teachers tend to:

    (a) be teaching, and get annoyed when you raise your hand to ask whether the principal can be a jerk;

    (b) escape to and hide in dark staff rooms when they aren't teaching;

    (c) say shifty, vague things like "Well, everyone has bad days…" but never get into details; and

(d) be very aware of the fact that principals can fire them.

So I have very little data on principals. My brother told me that his principal plays soccer with them but sometimes makes them sing too much. It is unclear whether encouraging children to sing qualifies as jerkish behavior.

At my friend's old school, kids got sent down to the office, where they had to sit on THE BENCH. THE BENCH was an uncomfortable stone bench where you sat, got a numb behind and worried about seeing the principal. But a bench isn't a jerkish thing. A bench is just a bench. Unless the principal left kids to sweat for a really long time on THE BENCH, I can't see how that made her a jerk.

I have to rely on scientific deduction for this one. Principals are generally human. They are not babies or toddlers. I have scientifically established that adult humans can be jerks and idiots. Therefore, principals can be jerks and idiots. I think a guy named Aristotle was the first one to come up with this kind of reasoning. But I believe I am the first scientist to apply it to the study of jerkology.

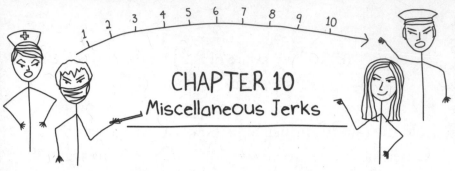

CHAPTER 10
Miscellaneous Jerks

The previous chapters have covered (in thorough scientific studies) most of the areas of life where jerks can be found. But there are still a few miscellaneous jerks left over who don't fit into the usual categories. Now, you might only run into these jerks once in a while, but in the interests of completeness, I thought they should be included and rated on the scale.

A) Nurses

Now, most of the nurses I've known have been fine (do I have to keep saying that?). The nurse I had when I had my tonsils out got me some after-hours ice cream and told me jokes. Like, what goes ha-ha-ha-PLOP? Somebody laughing their head off. Okay, kind of lame, but when you're green from anesthetic and your throat feels like it's on fire, it's good for a dry chuckle.

For every, say, few thousand nice, cheerful nurses, there will be a jerk nurse. Take our family doctor's office. I'm there with my mom, in the crowded waiting room, leafing through a ten-year-old

Sports Illustrated. The nurse calls my name. While my mom and I are putting down our magazines and getting up (literally taking two seconds), she calls my name again, sharply, like "this is the last time I will call this name!" Whoa, whoa, whoa…we've been waiting patiently, not snapping at anybody, for an appointment that was supposed to happen half an hour ago, and all of a sudden, because we're not sprinting to the desk, we get some attitude? Anyway, as she sees us, but we're still in the *crowded* waiting room, she rustles her papers and booms, "HE'S IN FOR WARTS? AGAIN??" First, I'm right here. Second, *lower your voice*. Third, I'm not *trying* to sprout these things, you know.

Rating: 7-8 (highly jerkish behavior)

B) Doctors and Dentists

My brother can't help having lousy teeth. I think it's something to do with his saliva, which is gross, but still, he can't help it. Anyway, he even had to have an operation on his jaw when he was only five years old. Sucks.

So he's lying there after the surgery with his face all pale and swollen like a chipmunk's. I thought we had the wrong kid at first, because he looked nothing like my brother Joe. I checked his hospital bracelet,

10

even though my parents seemed pretty sure it was him. Anyway, we were visiting early, before school and work. Not technically visiting hours, but the nurses made an exception.

In comes a group of doctors. They always seem to travel in herds. Herd is probably not right—what do you call a group of doctors? A pride? A clot? Anyway, all of these doctors swarm into the room. The main doctor, the guy that did the surgery, barks at the nurse, "Why are there all these people here?" like we're these random people who just wander from room to room staring at sick kids. Um, because we *love* this odd-looking chipmunk-child, you jerk.

He waves us aside, then starts his lecture to the group of student doctors. He asks them questions and then dumps all over the answers they give, because apparently he's *way* smarter than all of them. He leans over my brother, says "open up" and shines a light in his swollen mouth, and then he and the rest of them swarm off to annoy other sick children.

Now, I know the surgeon is busy, and I'm not expecting him to pull up a chair and say, "Hey, bud, how's the mouth? Let's talk." My brother wasn't in any shape for that. But how about using his name? Saying hello? Making me and my mom and dad feel like something other than furniture? Nope. That guy's probably got a very large brain, but he's not only an idiot; he's also a jerk.

Rating: 7-8 (total idiot tending to jerk)

C) Bus Drivers

I have often observed, in a casual, unscientific way, that some bus drivers, including school bus drivers, seem to hate kids. This observation is, admittedly, just based on some negative school field-trip experiences and one city bus ride. Hey, I'm the first one to admit that some kids can be annoying on the bus, but even if you're not bouncing on the seats, running in the aisles or sticking wads of gum under the seats, you sometimes look up to see the driver glaring at you in that big rearview mirror.

I walk to school, but I had my friend and research assistant Marcus observe his bus driver for a week. She sounds like a real jerk (again, many bus drivers *aren't*. Do I have to keep saying this?). I have to admit, when I handed Marcus a notepad with the words *Jerkish Behavior: Bus Drivers* written on it, I didn't expect much. Marcus isn't the most reliable guy in the world. I guess I expected that if he didn't forget about doing it, he would just lose the notepad. Was I ever wrong. He really threw himself into this project. Check out his list.

Jerkish Behavior: Bus Drivers
Elementary/Junior High Route 3C,
Monday to Friday

- pulling away from the curb and flooring it when J.M. was sprinting for the bus and all the kids on the bus were yelling, "Kid running! Kid running for the bus!"
- plowing through a red light, causing many other drivers to lay on their horns
- pulling the bus over and sitting there glaring at us and not starting up until we were **completely silent** (except for the girl in grade one who was crying and saying we'd be late for school)
- tossing an empty water bottle out the window!
- grabbing my shoulder because my music was too loud
- leaving us on the bus while she ran in to a convenience store to "get a coffee" (it was a pack of cigarettes—I saw it)
- forbidding two grade twos to sit together because they were **laughing too much**
- taking away S.V.'s cell phone because the ringtone was apparently "really annoying" (which it is, but so are the driver's sunglasses, but we can't just grab those)

This bus driver really seems to embrace the jerk lifestyle.

Rating: 9 (almost a complete jerk)

*****Update**: This driver has actually been fired! Not for all the jerkish things she did, but for not checking the bus and forgetting a grade-three kid, who was asleep. He had a great morning at the bus depot, eating his lunch and playing games on his iPod, but his parents were very angry about the whole thing. The new driver is much friendlier, but still wears those freaky, wraparound, bus-driver sunglasses.

D) Store Clerks

There's a convenience store near our junior high school, and we sometimes wander over at lunchtime to buy candy. Some kids, the complete jerks in the school, don't actually buy it—they steal it occasionally, or so I'm told. At least, that's why the store has implemented a new policy: only five junior high kids allowed in at one time, and you have to leave your backpacks, coats and boots at the door. Is that legal, I wonder? Anyway, it means we have to wait in line, freezing, until another kid leaves the store. Then we have to strip down and get wet socks, all for the privilege of giving them money for sour gummies.

The clerk, a guy who's been there for years, looks at you angrily as you go to pay.

"Is that it?" he asks suspiciously as you put down the gummies.

I'm in the middle of saying "looks like it" when he yells at another kid, "HEY! No going near the backpacks until AFTER you pay!"

Just another charming shopping experience. Some kids keep coming back to the store for the candy. Me? It's the service.

Rating: Junior high jerks who stole candy: 10 (complete jerks)

Rating: Rude store clerk: 4 (textbook idiot, but come to think of it, he's trying to make a living, and it must be stressful having to suspect every single kid, so maybe this can be downgraded to a 3)

E) Neighbors

Our neighbors on one side are really nice. We have keys to each other's houses, we look after each other's pets whenever anyone goes on vacation, we borrow ladders and sugar. It's a good arrangement.

The neighbors on the other side are very, very different. The Wicks are just plain miserable. They seem to spend their retirement staring out the window, just waiting to complain about balls that end up in their yard, kids on scooters or bikes who turn around in their driveway, or branches that slightly overhang their side of the property line. They're very, very concerned about that property line. I really didn't know what a property line was, but it appears to be an invisible line that separates their perfect lawn from our scrappy, dandelion-infested one. You know how when you're sitting in the back seat of a car and you run the side of your hand down the seat and tell your brother "here's the line" because his books and Lego are spilling into your space? That's kind of like a property line.

There's this two-foot-wide stretch of grass between the Wicks' driveway and our driveway. Literally, you can mow it by going once up and once down. Mr. Wicks has clearly measured and consulted with the city planners and stuff, because he only ever mows a *very narrow* strip of this grass. Not half. Maybe a quarter. So he has to position his mower mostly on his driveway to get his precise little strip done.

This seems like a very small thing. But don't you think that's a jerkish thing to do? When I mow the lawn, I always mow the whole strip. He mows, and he mows the four-inch strip of grass that he technically owns and not one blade more. It's very petty. But is it jerkish? Nah, it's such a small thing. It's not like he's throwing garbage our way, or having loud drunken parties every second night, or parking a monster sun-blocking, oil-leaking trailer in front of our house. In the interests of being nice and neighborly, I'll just classify Mr. Wicks as an idiot.

Rating: 5

F) Servers

When you are a child, people who serve you at restaurants generally leave you alone. They might ask you a few polite questions, but ultimately, they know somebody else is paying.

But when our family recently went out for dinner, the server did something that might qualify as jerkish behavior. He slapped down two kids' menus (the kind that double as your place mat and offer lame coloring opportunities and even lamer jokes) and a glass of crayons. Two menus, one for my eight-year-old brother and one for me. I'm thirteen. Not cool. How about a bib or a high chair? Are you going to offer those too? I declined coldly, making it clear I was *way* too mature for the

KIDS' MENU

chicken fingers
cheese pizza
macaroni and cheese
hot dog
all meals come with milk

tiny-tot food and the toddler word searches on the kids' menu.

Because I'm not sure if this is standard restaurant policy for everyone vaguely within the age range of the kids' menu or a deliberate choice on the part of the server, I'll give him the benefit of the doubt.

Rating: 3 (normal, tending slightly to idiot)

G) Internet Trolls

My brother Joe's grade-one class had a robin's nest in a shrub right outside their classroom window. The five blue eggs eventually hatched, and the class made a video of the ridiculously tiny, hungry little chicks. The teacher was so proud of the video that she added some lame music, recorded the class's reactions (you can clearly hear my brother saying excitedly, "Baby birds sure are baldies!") and posted it on YouTube. Anyway, cute, right? You would think so, but unbelievably, the video got some dislikes. Some big thumbs-down. What kind of jerk would do this?

I did some research, and this was not just an isolated, robin-hating Internet jerk. Many, many heartwarming animal videos online get a similar reaction. It might be a baby panda gumming bamboo for the first time, or a tiny kangaroo peeking out of its mother's pouch. Whatever animal it is, no matter how cute, innocent or uplifting the video, I guarantee that there will be some miserable Internet jerk ready to hate it. How could you officially "dislike" frolicking penguins? Or write negative, hateful comments about a big gorilla gently cuddling an adorable kitten?

These anonymous haters must really be in pretty bad shape if they have nothing better to do than complain about baby animals being cute or having fun. I'm not saying they have to say "Awww!" and forward them to their friends (if they have any). But here's an idea—maybe just don't seek out animal videos if you know you're really going to hate them.

Rating: 6-8 (jerk to almost complete jerk, depending on the level of hate)

CHAPTER 11
Once a Jerk, Always a Jerk?

Can jerks change their behavior and become regular, normal non-jerks? Or are they doomed to always be jerks? It's an interesting question in the study of jerkology.

Determined to get some scientific conclusions on this topic, I interviewed a former jerk, my uncle Dave. My mom, my grandparents and my uncle Tim all agree that Uncle Dave used to be a complete jerk. Even Dave agrees, as you'll see in the interview. But the interesting thing is that now he *isn't* a jerk. He's just normal. Why? How? Read this interview to find out.

***A note on technology:** I used an ancient tape recorder of my dad's for the interview, which involved pressing giant PLAY and RECORD buttons at the same time. My dad used to use it to record "rockin'" songs off the radio. Yeah, that'd be *great* sound quality, Dad. Anyway, it worked and everything, so the interview below is highly accurate. Bonus marks for use of ancient technology or historical artifacts? Possibly.

11

CASE STUDY #10
Interview with a Former Jerk

Subject: My uncle Dave

Laboratory: Saturday evening, the kitchen, our house

Experiment: Uncle Dave thought this was going to be a casual chat about a "difficult phase" of his childhood for some lame little school project I have. But I did my research and came prepared to get some answers.

Observations:

ME. So, Dave. Can I just call you Dave for this interview?

UNCLE DAVE. Nope. *Uncle* Dave to you, kid.

ME. So, Dave…Everyone agrees that you were a jerk as a kid. I mean *everyone*. Your sister, your brother, friends, cousins, neighbors. Your own parents even sort of sighed and nodded.

(*Uncle Dave swivels around to glare at my mom, who is chopping vegetables.*)

UNCLE DAVE. You got *Mom and Dad* in on this??

MOM (*laughing*). Hey, all in the name of science, Dave.

UNCLE DAVE (*looking uncomfortable*). Okay, okay. Look, I admit it. Many, many years ago, when I was very young, I was not, perhaps, an ideal child.

ME (*flipping through my notes*). Oh, you were a long way from being "ideal," Dave. I've interviewed several people, who told me about many, many jerkish things you did. Can you tell me about throwing Mom's doll down three flights of stairs?

UNCLE DAVE (*groaning*). This again? How many times do I have to say that I was seven years old and interested in *flight*! It was a scientific study, like this one...

MOM (*accusingly, chopping vegetables very hard now*). You were laughing and yelling "BOUNCE, DOLLY, BOUNCE!!!" You followed her down three flights, Dave! And cracked Miss Missy's hard plastic head!

UNCLE DAVE (*shrugging*). It was a cheap doll.

ME. How about when you let the air out of both of Uncle Tim's bike tires before his first day on his paper route?

UNCLE DAVE (*covering a smile*). Joke! That was a joke!

ME (*flipping through my notes*). Or prank-calling your grandma and grandpa until they had to get their number changed, or sprinkling weed killer all over the lawn so it died, or completely unraveling the living room rug, or throwing water bombs from the balcony at the girls at Mom's tenth birthday "garden party," or jumping out at little trick-or-treaters dressed as a seriously bloodied victim of an axe murderer with the axe still stuck in your head, or tying up a bunch of rocks in old clothes to make it look like there was a body at the bottom of the neighbor's pool—

UNCLE DAVE (*snatching my notebook and rifling through the pages*). You got that pool thing? How many…? Where did you…? Gee, I'd forgotten about most of these…

(*There is a long pause while Uncle Dave flips pages and reads. Actually, I shut off the tape recorder because there are many, many pages to get through. Finally he finishes and I press the giant PLAY and RECORD buttons again.*)

UNCLE DAVE (*sighing*). Okay, yes, I confess—I was a complete jerk. Thanks for documenting it all, kid. Your brother is now officially my favorite nephew.

ME. So, Dave. Why do you think you were a jerk then, and not now? Because everybody agrees that you're normal now.

MOM. I said *sort of* normal…

ME. Anyway, nobody thinks you're a jerk. I've almost never thought, "Hey, that Dave's a real jerk!"

UNCLE DAVE. *Uncle* Dave.

ME. Whatever.

UNCLE DAVE (*stretching his legs and settling back into his chair*). Why *was* I a jerk? I don't really know. Bored? Misunderstood? Needing some excitement and adventure? Too highly intelligent for the world around me?

MOM. Yeah, takes lots of brain power to throw a doll downstairs, Einstein.

UNCLE DAVE. Aren't we over that one yet? I'm sorry, okay? I'm very, very sorry about Miss Bitty.

MOM. Miss *MISSY*!

UNCLE DAVE (*looking bored*). Whatever.

ME. When did you stop being a jerk?

UNCLE DAVE (*sitting up*). Hey, that's actually interesting…when *did* I stop? I think I was probably about your age. What are you, about ten?

ME (*coldly*). I'm thirteen.

UNCLE DAVE. Yeah, yeah, I was probably about that. Why did I stop being a jerk? I don't know…We moved, switched schools, I started being a star on the sports teams…

MOM. And there was Trevor…

ME. Who's Trevor?

UNCLE DAVE. Uh, yeah, Trevor was an older kid who lived down the street. A *real* jerk. Made me look like an amateur. Actually, he became a low-level criminal when he hit his teens…Anyway, let's just say Trevor made me think about what a jerk I'd become. And where that could lead.

ME. So now you're not a jerk at all?

DAVE. Not even a little bit. Just a totally normal, good guy. Great uncle, great brother…

MOM. Well…

UNCLE DAVE (*getting up, reaching for the giant STOP button*). I think we're done here.

Conclusions: Uncle Dave seems to be living proof that even complete jerks can become regular non-jerks. In his case, it seemed to be his decision to stop being a jerk. But in the case of other jerks, becoming a non-jerk might be a result of the exhausting, thankless efforts of parents, teachers, counselors and possibly law-enforcement personnel. (See also Scientific Illustration #3: The Path to Complete Jerkdom.)

It remains unclear *why* jerks change their behavior. Uncle Dave wasn't very helpful there. He seemed to say that a change of scene, new interests and becoming aware of other jerks were all factors. Possibly, being avoided or called a jerk might start to register on some jerks and cause them to do a bit of reflecting.

Uncle Dave shut off the tape recorder and left quickly before I asked the last question, which was "Do you still have episodes of jerkish behavior?" So who knows?

CHAPTER 12
Can Animals Be Jerks?

Until now, this project has focused exclusively on human jerks. But is the quality of being a jerk limited to humans? Is jerkishness something at which only we as a species excel? Is it related to our bigger-than-many-animals brain size, or our ability to plan?

In this chapter, I expand the research to other species and draw some important scientific conclusions about the question "Can animals be jerks?" Let me say right now that I'm not including this chapter only to bump up my word count and make this quite an astonishingly long and thorough science project. No, the study of whether animals can be jerks seems a logical, necessary next step in the study of jerkishness.

This was a very hard chapter to research. I mean, think about it. *Animals.* There are a lot of them out there. Our family dog, Daisy, was an obvious subject for study, but she's the happiest, laziest, least jerkish creature I've ever known. If anybody ever does a study involving gulping food or lying in sunbeams, Daisy's your dog. I had to really hunt around for some interesting case studies.

12

A) Pets

Ever strolled through a pet store? There are millions of possible pets to study. It could be a whole project on its own, with chapters on goldfish, hamsters and gerbils. And I'm not even including birds and reptiles. Or exotic pets, like those nine-thousand-dollar birds with curling black tongues and gray reptiley feet. Or monster snakes. Or chinchillas. No, I had to draw the line somewhere, which was made easier by the fact that none of my friends have anything more exciting than cats and dogs.

CASE STUDY #11
The Flyer-Route Monster

Subject: Rosie the St. Bernard

Laboratory: The front yard of 887 Fairlee Way, a house on my flyer route

Experiment: 887 Fairlee Way is better known as Rosie's house. Rosie is a monster St. Bernard with a huge, drooly mouth the size and dampness of a half watermelon. She seems a friendly enough dog until you lay a finger on the front gate to, say, try to deliver a flyer. As soon as she sees you touch the gate, Rosie starts up this deep growling, a rumbling like a huge truck in a tunnel. So you freeze. You try again.

Same growl. You look into her droopy, red-rimmed monster eyes. You figure it's not worth it and 887 Fairlee Way never, ever gets a flyer.

My cousins Jake and Elizabeth (who have three dogs) volunteered to be research assistants in this experiment to see if they could deliver the flyer at Rosie's house. "You need to be firm. Alpha dog," said Jake.

Observations: My cousin Jake's kind of pushy, and if he hadn't been helping me out, the way he just snatched the flyer from me might be annoying. Maybe even jerk-like. Anyway, he grabs the flyer, confidently opens the gate and walks right in. Rosie skips the growl and heads straight into deafening barking while she gallops straight at Jake. Jake moves pretty quickly, let me tell you. He gets out and we shut and lock the gate just before Rosie slams into it from the other side.

When it's Elizabeth's turn, she makes me and Jake cross the street so we won't "crowd" Rosie. "You need to *understand* her," Elizabeth says, picking up the flyer that Jake dropped. We hear her talking to Rosie gently in this singsongy voice. "Who's a good girl, Rosie? Are *you* a good girl? Nice dog. Nice dog…" She lays a hand on the gate, and Rosie lumbers to her feet, growling and with hackles raised.

Rosie's owner, a tiny old lady, finally opens the door. She snaps, "Rosie! Sit!" and Rosie, with an adoring look, sits, her tail thumping happily. The lady turns to us. "Sorry, kids. She's so protective. But she's just a big pup, really." She pats Rosie, who rolls onto her back, closes her eyes and drools happily.

Conclusions: Rosie is not a jerk. This sort of surprised me. I thought at the beginning of this case study that she might be. She's a monster. She's scary. She freaks out easily. But she's just protecting her house and her tiny old lady. The old lady isn't even a jerk. She clearly didn't train Rosie to be all aggressive. It's something Rosie must have figured out for herself in her little dog brain.

No way, no how am I ever delivering a flyer at Rosie's house.

CASE STUDY #12
The Four-Pound Ankle-Biter

Subject: Peaches, a tiny white dog with a ponytail tied on the top of her head with a pink ribbon

Laboratory: My house

Experiment: My mom has a friend from work named Sheila. Sheila doesn't have kids or anything.

She just has Peaches. She and Peaches were over after school one day when Joe and I came home.

Now, Peaches is adorable and tiny. Her paws are the size of quarters, and she has very silky fur and a tiny pink tongue. My brother and I love dogs, so we were kind of excited. Here's how it went.

Observations:

JOE. Awww, she's so cute. (*Drops down onto his knees, holding out his hand.*)

PEACHES. RAR-RAR-RAR-RAR-RAR-RAR-RAR-RAR-RAR-RAR-RAR-RAR! (*This bark is very quick and aggressive and it goes on and on. There're only so many times you can type RAR.*)

SHEILA. Peaches! Baby girl, calm down, sweetie! (*She dives for the dog, just as it lunges at Joe's hand, and grabs Peaches by her pink studded collar.*) She just gets excited with people she doesn't know. Wants to give them smoochies. Doesn't she? Doesn't my little one? (*Struggles to hold her.*)

PEACHES. RAR-RAR-RAR-RAR-RAR-RAR-RAR-RAR-RAR-RAR-RAR-RAR!

ME (*nervously stepping away from Peaches, who has slipped out of Sheila's cuddle and who starts jumping as high as my head while snapping her tiny jaws*). Whoa, hey, down, girl!

SHEILA. Sweet pea, *down*, love.

PEACHES. RAR-RAR-RAR-RAR-RAR-RAR-RAR-RAR-RAR-RAR-RAR-RAR!

ME. Wow, she's little but she sure is… AAAAAAHHHHHH!

The "AAAAAAHHHHHH" is me getting bitten on the ankle by some impossibly sharp, tiny teeth. Taking a hit for science is how I look at it. Long story short. Sheila scoops up Peaches and disappears while I bleed on the carpet and Mom hunts for the stuff that stings like crazy but prevents death by dog bite.

Conclusions: While Peaches sure has some aggression issues and might benefit from a training class or an animal psychologist, if I remain scientifically objective I just can't call her a jerk.

Biting my ankle might have been slightly jerkish, but was she deliberately trying to be irritating or annoying or hurtful?

I don't think so.

She was just acting on instinct. She was probably just having her tiny aggro-dog fun. She was just being Peaches. Little dogs can be scarier than big dogs.

The Night Screamer

Subject: My friend Gus's orange cat, Scooter. Who names a fifty-pound cat Scooter? People who name a kid Gus, I guess.

Laboratory: Gus's house on a sleepover

Experiment: Gus was interested in this science project and volunteered Scooter as a subject for study. Scooter had other plans. He was completely uninterested in being studied and did as little as possible that whole afternoon. He lumbered from food bowl to couch, slept and then had a snack and another nap. Seriously, why don't cats live forever if all they do is eat and sleep? "Oh, Scooter's on a different schedule than the rest of us," laughed Gus's mom. She wasn't kidding.

Observations: Cut to the middle of the night, when I wake in a sweat to hideous screaming. Gus is snoring in the bunk above me. His parents are snoring in the room down the hall. The wailing and screaming go on and on. I am almost convinced that two people have broken into the house just so that one can murder the other.

I shake Gus awake. He listens for a second, mumbles "It's only Scooter" and puts his pillow over his head.

Only Scooter. After screaming (At what? At who?) for about four hours, Scooter pounds up and down the stairs, plays hockey with a jingling cat toy up and down the hall (a game that apparently never gets old), barfs up a disgusting hairball, has a hissing/spitting fight with the dog and scratches endlessly on the bedroom furniture. He sits on my head for what's left of the night, batting at my hair.

Conclusions: I am so completely professional that even though Scooter cost me a night of sleep, and my eyes are crossing as I type this, I still don't think he is a jerk.

This is interesting, because during the night I called Scooter many, many names, including "jerk." Turns out I didn't really mean it.

Again, animals don't really *mean* to be jerks. They're either acting on instinct or doing things randomly or for fun. They're batting a fun ball or pawing at a fun face or biting an ankle just for fun. They haven't decided to be mean. They haven't planned.

Final conclusion: Pets can't be jerks.

B) Wild Animals

Perhaps there is something about pets being relatively tame (even if they're badly trained) that prevents them from being complete jerks. I wondered if *wild* animals, animals that play by nature's rules, behave differently. We've all seen the nature shows with the disturbing footage of the lions that deliberately target the weakest, slowest antelope (and despite our fevered, incoherent mental urgings to "Run, GO, just RUN!" usually get them), and the ugly hyenas that move in and bicker over the disgusting remains. That is nature. That's how it works. Can we possibly see elements of jerkitude in that?

Now, much as I would have liked to track a bear, cougar or wolf for this project, I was limited by time, availability and personal safety. So I studied another, more common (though still wild) animal.

CASE STUDY #14
The Garbage Thieves

You might be thinking, "Garbage thieves? Who cares who steals *garbage*? It's *garbage*." True, but these thieves scatter and smear the garbage they don't actually want to eat all over the driveway, and I have to clean it up, so, yeah, I care.

Subject: Magpies
Laboratory: The end of our driveway, Monday evening (garbage collection Tuesday morning)

Experiment: This was a very spontaneous case study. I came into the living room to see my mom looking out the front window. "Those jerks are ripping up the garbage again," she said. *Jerks?* I was on the case.

Observations: I slip out the door very quietly to observe the magpies. They couldn't care less that I am there—those week-old carrot peelings and moldy pizza crusts are obviously good eats. While I watch, they really attack the bag, using their huge beaks and gnarly claws to toss out old tea bags, used tissues, apple cores and ancient spaghetti.

As the mess on the driveway widens, I call, "Hey, stop it!" The magpies turn their heads slightly, stare at me with their cold bird eyes and turn back to vandalizing our garbage. "Stop it," I repeat, remembering that even though I have no killer beak or wicked claws, I am still way bigger than they are. I walk over. They hop away, but only a few hops. Casual, assessing hops. "Are you serious?" hops. Then one of them shrieks *AA-AA-AA*, which is probably something like "get lost, loser" in magpie. Although, come to think of it, that's the only sound they *ever* make.

"GO. AWAY," I say, stamping my feet and waving my arms and trying to look bigger. They look at me in disgust and fly a few feet up to the roof, where they sit looking down at me. *AA-AA-AA*. They call their friends, and several other magpies settle on our roof, *AA-AA-AA*-ing their heads off. The second I move away from the garbage, one of the birds flies in, which is humiliating and annoying.

I am pretty much surrounded by big, aggressive, determined birds. I stand there staring them down and defending our garbage for several ridiculous minutes. Then I realize that they are just waiting for me to give up. It seems like they know I have homework and hockey practice. And garbage cleanup.

They fly down and settle into their interrupted garbage picking before I've taken maybe six steps back to the house, which is the first time I think, "These birds are real jerks." The second time I think it, I'm picking up old hot-dog buns smeared with ketchup and laundry lint and trying not to gag.

Conclusions: This was the hardest case study of the whole project. All the others seemed to point to some obvious conclusions, but even though both my mom and I described the birds as jerks, were they really? Or were we just using the word *jerk* unscientifically?

I did some research (research *within* a case study? Is this guy an out-of-control science geek or what?) and found that magpies actually have very big brains behind those creepy, cold eyes. Like, monkey-smart brains. Recognize-yourself-in-a-mirror brains. Figure-out-how-to-use-a-twig-to-get-a-longer-stick-to-get-food-out-of-a-box brains. Planner brains. But even though this kind of intelligence rivals that of some of my classmates, apparently magpies are considered to think at the level of a young child. Of course, it's humans, not magpies, who are doing the measuring. Anyway, conclusions:

Like small children, magpies probably can't form the intent or do the planning required for true jerkish activity. I'm saying "probably," not "definitely."

Further research into their behavior (their morning screeching, their destructiveness, their bullying of other birds) might move them very, very close to being legitimately labeled jerks.

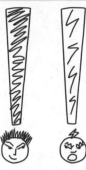

CHAPTER 13
You Be the Jerk!

I think we've learned a lot from these many, many typed pages. Wow, *thirteen* chapters (fourteen including the concluding one), nine scientific illustrations and fourteen case studies! I'd call that impressive.

In this chapter, we relax and kick back with a little skill-testing fun (and hopefully some bonus marks). This end-of-report exercise is called "You Be the Jerk!" You know something is going to be fun when it ends in an exclamation point!

Many normal people can spot jerkish behavior when it happens and even unconsciously rate it on their internal Jerk-O-Meter. But to truly grasp the many elements of jerkosity, you have to put yourself in the jerk's shoes. You have to *think* like a jerk in order to understand jerkish behavior, if not the jerks themselves. This exercise may appear fun and simple, but it really illustrates the immense scientific value in being able to predict jerkish behavior. Because (and this is really a profound question), if you could anticipate the way a jerk might act, could you prevent it or at least avoid it?

13

Normal people attempting this exercise may not do very well, which is probably a good thing. Other people may get top marks, and, well, you jerks know who you are.

You Be the Jerk! Quiz

So the idea here is pretty simple. You pretend to be the jerk in each question and select the kind of idiotic or jerkish things you might do in a given situation.

1) You're an adult looking for a parking spot in a crowded lot. You:
   (a) park properly between the lines in a normal spot
   (b) squeeze into a spot that's too small, so the people next to you have to climb through the back of their van to get in and out
   (c) whip into an empty spot just ahead of an older, slower driver who's clearly aiming for the same one and who technically was there first
   (d) park at an angle using up two spots, because you don't want anyone touching your car

(e) pull into the disabled parking spot even though those big signs are hard to miss

2) You're a junior high student. You see a kid you know up ahead with a Red Wings ballcap on. You:
   (a) catch up with him and have a good-natured talk about favorite teams
   (b) yell "Red Wings suck!" but in the kind of conversation-opener way that junior high boys understand
   (c) ridicule his choice of team to the point where it isn't funny *at all*
   (d) flick the cap off his head just to see him flail to catch it
   (e) pick the cap up and fling it into a nearby tree

3) You're an office worker. You don't bring anything to the office party, but you:
   (a) compliment everyone else's cooking
   (b) pretend you've helped in other ways by rearranging furniture or bringing some music
   (c) stand around and eat the food everyone else has brought, including *all* of the smoked salmon dip

(d) talk loudly about how wasteful staff parties are

(e) laugh about how much money you saved by not bringing anything

4) You're a parent waiting to pick up your child from school. You:

    (a) park quietly down the street where parents are supposed to park

    (b) park in the bus zone right in front of the school so your little darling doesn't have to walk six more feet

    (c) run your car for the full half an hour that you wait, so that the grade-three teachers have to shut the windows to keep the exhaust fumes out

    (d) light up a cigarette just as your child gets in the car

    (e) flick the cigarette butt (and your breath-freshening gum wrapper) out the car window on your way home

5) You're a grade-two student. At "sharing time," one of your classmates is telling a new joke she learned. You:

(a) listen attentively because you also like a good joke

(b) sort of listen, but focus more on picking some old gum off the bottom of a nearby desk

(c) get into a scuffle with another kid on the polka-dot mat because you consider the blue dot your own personal property

(d) yell "BO-RING!" as the joke teller launches into it

(e) if you've heard the joke before, blurt out the punch line before the joke teller gets to it

6) Your school's fire alarm goes off. The school is evacuating onto the front lawn (like that's not going to be a scorcher of a place when the fire really takes off). Anyway, you:

(a) file out in single file, quick-walking in an orderly fashion

(b) break into a trot and jockey to butt into the front of the line

(c) two-hand push other kids in the back to get to the nearest door

(d) scream "Fire! FIRE! We're all going to DIE!"

(e) lie when they find out that it was you who pulled the alarm in the first place

7) You're in gym class. It's the swimming unit, so you:
   (a) enjoy the harmless aquatic exercise and the break from the smell of the school gym
   (b) crowd up against other kids in line for the slide, because other kids probably don't mind that when they're nearly naked
   (c) tell the scared kids that there have been reports of a shark in the deep end
   (d) dunk other kids unexpectedly when the teacher isn't looking so they get that raw, bleachy-burny feeling in their nose, mouth and throat
   (e) dive deep and pretend to be the shark, targeting the scared kids' legs

8) You're the teacher in the gym class above. You:
   (a) pretend that the swimming unit is actually going to be fun for more than, say, three strong swimmers
   (b) enforce the pre-swim shower rule, then keep kids shivering and blue-lipped on the side of the pool while you explain obvious safety measures for half an hour
   (c) let the lifeguards look out for potential drowners while you text your boyfriend

(d) make everyone do endless lung-inflaming
   lengths
(e) make everyone go off the high diving board
   (even those kids who might be afraid of
   heights or depths or sharks)

9) You're a kid at recess. When the bell rings, you:
   (a) return promptly to the school and change
      into your indoor shoes so as not to muddy
      the school's floors
   (b) return promptly to the school, smearing
      muddy streaks all the way to your classroom
   (c) steal the ball the other kids were playing
      with and run into the school
   (d) stash the ball in your backpack before they
      can find it
   (e) when the other kids tell on you, lie to
      the teacher and then the principal about
      what happened and accuse *the other kids* of
      bullying *you*

10) It's picture day at your school. You:
   (a) smile nicely for both your personal picture
      and the class picture
   (b) mess up your picture so you can miss class
      again when the retakes come around

(c) smile nicely for your picture and then make loud rude noises so that the kids getting photographed after you jump and look alarmed in their pictures

(d) smile nicely for your picture, then open your mouth hideously for the class picture

(e) smile nicely for your picture, then make rabbit ears on the two kids beside you in the class pictures so that they look back years later and think, "What a jerk"

You Be the Jerk! Scoring Key

Here's the cool part about this test—you grade yourself! Or not, because it's just for fun. Sweet, I know.

This is how it works, for all you try-hard keeners who'll actually take the time to do it. You may already have guessed that the answers in the quiz generally go from being normal (a) to being a complete jerk (e). We give each letter a number rating (see the chart at right)—the higher the number, the bigger the jerk. If you selected more than one answer to a question, add 'em up (which will pretty much guarantee complete jerk numbers).

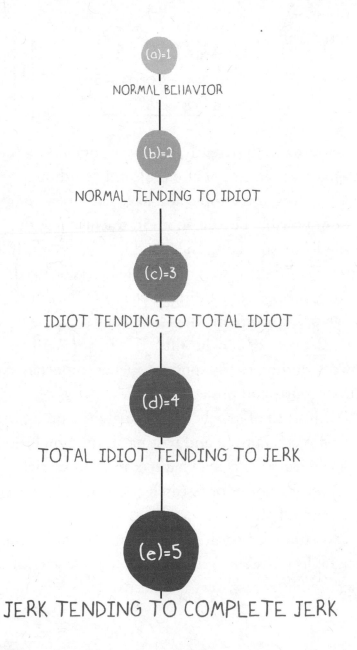

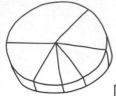

CHAPTER 14
Drawing Some Conclusions
(and a Cool Pie Chart)

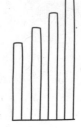

It is important, apparently, to have a concluding paragraph at the end of any project. Even though you might be sick of the topic and have said everything that can possibly be said about it, teachers *love* the concluding paragraph. They tend to dock marks if you don't write and write and write a decent-sized, multi-sentenced concluding paragraph. They like the wrapping-it-up, making-it-all-sound-sort-of-finished aspect of conclusions. This is, apparently, why concluding paragraphs are seen as important for essays, reports and projects.

But instead of lamely and boringly recapping the entire project, cutting and pasting all the conclusions I made during the other chapters and summarizing the massive amount of research I've done, I think I'll do something different.

Even though I've already written two concluding paragraphs (see above), I still have one last scientific diagram that is very, very conclusive.

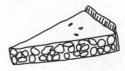

Scientific Illustration #9: The Very Last One: The Elements of Jerkish Behavior

We have seen in this project many different examples of jerkish behavior. But though the behavior of jerks is as varied as that of non-jerkish people, jerks have several things in common. My research has revealed certain elements that are common to almost all observable jerkish behavior:

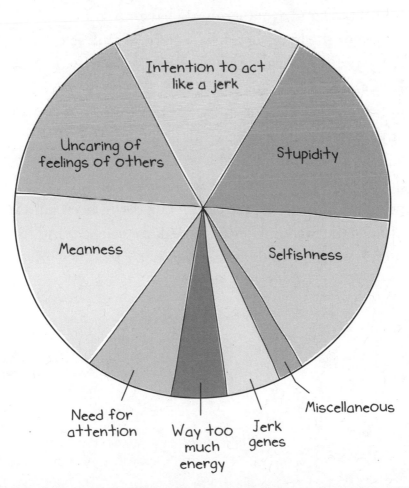

Can you end a project on a pie chart?

Probably not.

My concluding and very final observation is that as long as there are humans on this planet, some of them will be jerks. There were, there are, there probably always will be jerks. We know them when we see them, and scientific studies such as this one can take us beyond gut reactions and help us identify, classify, understand and avoid jerkish behavior.

As for the jerks themselves, I don't think science can ever fully explain why jerks behave as they do. It might be a combination of genetics, intelligence, upbringing and opportunity. Or there may not be any reason at all for why a jerk acts like a jerk. There will be those non-jerks who wonder if society has done something to make jerks so angry, annoying and motivated. Have we, the caring non-jerks, been guilty of misunderstanding jerks? I speak for science, and for pretty much anybody who's ever met a jerk, when I say *nah*—it's all on the jerks.

ACKNOWLEDGMENTS

Thanks to the wonderful staff at Orca, especially
Sarah "Giggle-Snort" Harvey for effortlessly channeling
her inner thirteen-year-old boy while editing, and
Jenn Playford and Chantal Gabriell for bringing their
formidable and playful creativity to the illustrations
and design. Thanks also to another creative soul, my
sister Jen, for appreciating and encouraging all the
story ideas I throw at her. And finally, thanks to my
children, Kate, Ben and Sam, for their keen jerk-radar,
which I think will serve them well.

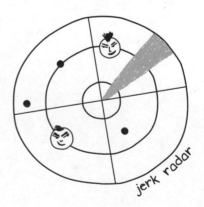

jerk radar

Alison Hughes is an award-winning writer who has lived, worked and studied in Canada, England and Australia. She was introduced to the world of jerks as a young child when her swimming instructor pushed her off the diving board into the deep end/shark tank. She has been wary of jerks (and deep water) ever since. She lives with her family in Edmonton, where snoring dogs provide the soundtrack to her writing.